Nobody
knows you
when you're
down... and
dead.

Also by Jill Churchill

Grace and Favor Series
ANYTHING GOES
IN THE STILL OF THE NIGHT

Jane Jeffry Series
GRIME AND PUNISHMENT
A FAREWELL TO YARNS
A QUICHE BEFORE DYING
THE CLASS MENAGERIE
A KNIFE TO REMEMBER
FROM HERE TO PATERNITY
SILENCE OF THE HAMS
WAR AND PEAS
FEAR OF FRYING
THE MERCHANT OF MENACE
A GROOM WITH A VIEW
MULCH ADO ABOUT NOTHING

Jill Churchill can be contacted at
Cozybooks@earthlink.net or through her website
www.JillChurchill.com.

JILL CHURCHILL

SOMEONE
TO
WATCH
OVER
ME

AVON BOOKS
An Imprint of HarperCollinsPublishers

This is a work of fiction. Names, characters, places, and incidents are products of the author's imagination or are used fictitiously and are not to be construed as real. Any resemblance to actual events, locales, organizations, or persons, living or dead, is entirely coincidental.

AVON BOOKS
An Imprint of HarperCollins*Publishers*
10 East 53rd Street
New York, New York 10022-5299

Copyright © 2001 The Janice Brooks Trust
Excerpts copyright © 1999, 2000, 2001, 2002 by The Janice Brooks Trust
ISBN: 0-06-103123-2
www.avonmystery.com

First Avon Books paperback printing: September 2002
First William Morrow hardcover printing: December 2001

Avon Trademark Reg. U.S. Pat. Off. and in Other Countries, Marca Registrada, Hecho en U.S.A.
HarperCollins ® is a registered trademark of HarperCollins Publishers Inc.

Printed in the U.S.A.

10 9 8 7 6 5 4 3 2 1

With enormous gratitude to Jeane Westin
who graciously gave me a copy
of her marvelous book
Making Do: How Women Survived the '30s

SOMEONE
TO
WATCH
OVER
ME

Chapter 1

{Late July, 1932}

Lily Brewster and her brother, Robert, sat in the dining room of the mansion known as Grace and Favor Cottage. Robert was at the head of the long table reading the *New York Times* and mumbling to himself as he sipped his morning coffee and grimaced. "Lily, is Mrs. Prinney watering this stuff down? It hasn't got any taste."

"I think she is. She said something chirpy about chicory tasting just like coffee." Lily nearly had to shout to be heard at the other end. Lily was, as usual, doing the household books and had receipts, scrap paper, pencil, and pen spread around her while she munched on her toast with her left hand.

Between them, halfway along, was their boarder, Phoebe Twinkle, the dainty young red-headed village milliner and seamstress. "Where is Mrs. Prinney?" she said, touching a napkin to her lips.

"Gardening. As usual," Lily said.

She closed her ledger and capped her late mother's fountain pen, tidied up her piles of paperwork, picked up her plate and silverware, and went to sit between the others so she didn't have to scream to be heard.

"Should this be worrying us, Robert? Or is she just taking up a new hobby?"

Robert, who was seldom without a grin and a smart crack, was uncharacteristically solemn. "Haven't you been to the greengrocer's lately? There's almost nothing there except what that local woman grows."

"But not even Roxanne Anderson can possibly grow enough for the whole town," Phoebe put in.

"The farmer can't buy enough seeds or hire help," Robert went on. "The middleman can't afford to ship produce around the country, and that hurts the railroads. Dominoes falling. Or a downward spiral, if you want to look at it that way."

Lily had been working hard at trying (but failing) to ignore the country's deteriorating financial situation. She ran her hands through her hair and admitted, "I hate this. It just gets worse and worse. Thank goodness the Democrats have nominated Governor Roosevelt for President. At least he can't make more of a mess of the economy than Hoover."

"Unless it completely collapses before he takes

office—if he wins," Robert added. "The election is months away, and the new President doesn't take office until next March. Anything could happen by then."

"You think Hoover could be reelected?" Lily asked in alarm.

Robert looked at his sister and realized he'd frightened her more than he should have. Not that he wasn't terrified. While President Hoover made weekly announcements of how the economy was improving, it was obvious that everyday life for almost everyone was getting much, much worse. "No, Governor Roosevelt will be elected. He's the only governor who's actually done demonstrably good things for his own state. He's beaten the state legislature into funding a few public works projects. Now I've got to change clothes for my own project."

"And what's that?" Lily asked.

"With Mr. Prinney's permission I hired a couple of young men from the village, the Harbinger boys, to help me tear down the old icehouse. There's some good sturdy wood in it that someone could put to use."

"The icehouse? How will we cool things?" Lily asked.

"Not the one behind the pantry," Robert said, rolling his eyes. "The one in the woods."

Lily looked at him as if he were mad.

"You don't believe me?" Robert said. "Come take a look."

"No can do," Lily said. "Phoebe and I are on our way to a special meeting of the VLL."

"The VLL?"

"Robert, how could you forget?" Lily said. "The Voorburg Ladies League. It's the first meeting I've been invited to. It's quite an honor and might mean the village is accepting us as real people."

Robert made an exaggerated motion of slapping his head. "Stupid of me," he said sarcastically. "How can you bear to be around that White woman who runs it?"

Phoebe and Lily exchanged a look; Phoebe answered. "She's not really so bad when you get to know her."

Robert waved this away. "I've met her. To my sorrow. She's a runaway locomotive."

"But I hear she means well, Robert," Lily objected. "Her manner is bossy, but people say her ideas are usually good. She just got back from a visit to Philadelphia and told Phoebe she's had a brainstorm about how we can help others in Voorburg. An emergency meeting. Phoebe, are you ready to go?"

The two young women gathered their handbags and the canvas bag with their good shoes and set out to take the shortcut through the woods and down the hill to town. Though there wasn't much traffic on the road, it wound around so much that it was at least four times the length of the old Indian path from the hills overlooking the river.

They would change from their sturdy shoes to their nice ones once they were close to the village of Voorburg-on-Hudson. Phoebe had alerted Lily that Mrs. White was obsessed with appearances, and while they wouldn't admit it to Robert, neither of them wanted to be accused of bad taste in footwear. Especially not by Mrs. White, who was always immaculately dressed, thoroughly corseted—and well shod.

Phoebe Twinkle, who had been in Voorburg longer than Lily and seldom had access to an automobile, was much more surefooted on the steep path than Lily, but she held back with good grace and set her pace to her companion's.

"I don't really know very much about Mrs. White except that she scares me to death," Lily said to Phoebe. "Has she lived here long?"

"All her life, as far as I know," Phoebe said, pulling aside a branch of a decrepit maple that really should be trimmed. "My former landlady talks about knowing her since childhood—Mrs. White's childhood, not my landlady's."

Phoebe, whose main claim to fame was that she made hats for Mrs. Franklin D. Roosevelt, had rented her millinery shop from a recently widowed woman who went to live with her sister and let Phoebe live in a furnished room above the shop. But the landlady made so many inroads into the belongings she'd left behind that Phoebe was at her wits' end when Lily offered her one of the many rooms at Grace and Favor Cottage for her own.

The move meant she had to walk to work down the hill instead of just down the stairs, but the food at Grace and Favor was better than Mabel's cafe and so was the company.

She and the other women in the mansion—Lily, Mrs. Prinney, and Mimi Smith, the house-keeper—had adjusted well to communal living by being polite and friendly, but not going out of their way to interfere in each other's private lives and interests except in emergency situations. Mimi cleaned like a demon and helped in the kitchen when Mrs. Prinney asked her to, but she kept to herself, in what little free time she had, in the third-floor room down the hall from Phoebe's larger room. This was where Phoebe did her other job, sewing and repairing clothes for local ladies.

Lily took care of the household finances and constantly huddled with Elgin Prinney, Esquire, who was executor of the estate Lily and Robert would inherit after they served their ten years at Grace and Favor. Lily had become a fanatic penny-pincher after their father had lost the for-merly vast family fortune in the Crash of 1929 and had to live in utter poverty until Mr. Prinney found them. Lily was determined to know every-thing about the vast holding of properties Great-uncle Horatio had left to them.

Mrs. Prinney did the cooking. The Prinneys' four daughters were grown and married, and she was pleased to be cooking for a crowd again. But her sudden spurt of obsessive vegetable gardening this past spring worried Lily. In the year—almost—since she and Robert moved here, Mrs. Prinney could get food of such good quality that Lily half wondered about the portly older woman's true relationships with the Voorburg butcher and greengrocer. Now she was growing beans, carrots, broccoli, and celery, not to mention horseradish, and canning the produce like mad nearly all night, when it was cooler in the kitchen.

"Do you have any idea what Mrs. White has discovered? Why this is a special meeting?" Lily asked, as they approached town and sat on a flat slab of granite behind the defunct bank to change their shoes.

Phoebe shook her head and shrugged. "But it must be good. She's never called a meeting before on such short notice and with so much insistence."

Robert looked over the old icehouse deep in the woods beside the mansion while he waited for the two workers who were going to tear it down. There was very good wood in it—good enough to repair homes and even possibly make some furniture from the better pieces. The workers, brothers Harry and Jim Harbinger, would get the benefit, since the icehouse hadn't been used for years, and this was a waste not, want not society these days.

He tried the door and found it locked. Glancing

around for a likely spot for a key to be hidden, he heard the two young men approaching. "I guess we're going to have to take the hinges off the door," he said, when they got closer.

"We could break it down," Jim, the younger one, said.

His brother Harry cuffed him. "And wreck the wood? Mama would smack you to Cincinnati if she heard you say that."

Harry put his heavy toolbox down on the ground and laid out several items: a short pry bar, a couple of screwdrivers that looked to be fifty years old, and three hammers in different weights.

Fortunately, the hinges were on the outside. The older brother stuck a screwdriver in the lower hinge and pounded at it with the smallest hammer. After a moment, the hinge was free. He did the same with the lower one, and all three men stood in front of the door to lower it to the ground.

A musty smell wafted over them. Robert lighted a flashlight and shone it into the window-less icehouse.

"*Holy Toledo!* There's a body!" he exclaimed.

Chapter 2

One thing nobody could claim accurately about Edith White was that she was a snob. She expected women to dress in their best, but she also understood that "best" for some was a flexible measure.

She was glad not to have suffered as much from the Depression as many others, just as deserving as she. Her present husband, Henry, had a good job supervising a chain of insurance agencies and had made sensible investments in property. Her first husband, Bernard, likewise had been well-to-do, though he wasn't the cheerful man Henry was. Bernard had been a smart and tough-minded expert in livestock concerns in the stock market. He made excellent consulting fees with brokerage firms. So when she was widowed at thirty-nine, she had a financially comfortable life.

In her mid-forties now, she looked older. A tall, portly woman, she wore very good clothes, but they looked like they'd been passed down for a couple of generations and, though of excellent quality and in good condition, they were out-of-date. Her expensive shoes were primarily practical lace-up oxfords with sturdy heels. Most of her clothing budget must have gone to the best, most confining corsets available. Hips flattened, bosom upthrust, her figure was impressive. Her fair and only slightly graying hair was always in place, marcelled into perfect waves and lacquered to her head. She always wore a stylish but practical hat made by Phoebe Twinkle.

The efforts she probably had once lavished upon the orphaned child of her first husband's sister were now aimed at her community instead. She believed, as did President Hoover, that charity begins (and ends) at home. Unlike the President, however, she was always careful to not call it charity but rather "a little help."

She made a visible effort to be friendly and casual and insisted on being addressed as "Edith" in the privacy of the meetings. She spoke of her husband as "Henry" to the members of the Voorburg Ladies League, as few upper-crust women would have done, except with close friends. In public, of course, he was Mr. White.

But for all her native kindness, she was a magnificent force of nature. She seemed to feel she always knew the "right" thing to do and could never be talked out of her views. Edith White had organized people all her life, often saying, "It's for their own good."

And it usually was.

The Voorburg Ladies League had started out as a sewing club in mid-1930. Edith solicited donations, somewhat brutally, from everyone who could spare an outgrown suit or dress or bed or table linens. Before the weekly meeting, she'd have her maid wash the donated items, and Edith herself cut the fabric from these old topcoats, cotton blouses, table runners, and napkins to exact four-and-a-half-inch squares, laid them out by color and texture, and the VLL turned them into quilts and coverlets for the poor.

Edith White was suspected of buying the batting, backing, and thread, though she pretended that they were also donations from some mysterious source who didn't wish to be named.

She was the ultimate clubwoman, a new breed of female who believed a woman's thoughts and efforts counted as much as any man's. This shocked and dismayed most men and some women.

As Lily and Phoebe sat and changed their shoes, Lily said, "I've run across Mrs. White at church and have an idea of what she's like. Is there anything I should know about the other women in the club? I don't want to say anything tactless."

"You wouldn't anyway," Phoebe replied. "Susan Gasset works at the movie house, and her sister takes care of her children in the evenings. Susan's my favorite of the group. Nina Pratt is a hairdresser; she has a shop at the back of her house. And you know Peggy Rismiller."

"The Episcopal minister's wife," Lily said, with a nod.

"Roxanne Anderson is also a part of the group."

"Mrs. Prinney mentions her often," Lily said, "but I don't think I've met her."

"The newest member besides you is Ruby Heggan," Phoebe went on. "She's also the youngest and has a darling baby. We better get moving. Edith doesn't like us to be tardy."

"Phoebe," Edith White said, when the two young women from Grace and Favor arrived, "I've given you the loosest fabric, because I know you can handle it better than most."

Then she explained to Lily that within this meeting of the circle of women, they went by their first names. Though naturally they wouldn't do so otherwise.

"Phoebe already told me that, Mrs.—er, Edith." How social rules were changing, Lily thought. Her mother would be tossing fretfully in her grave if she could hear her well-brought-up daughter addressing an older woman by her first name.

Edith assigned Lily, who admitted she wasn't much of a needlewoman, some of the more sturdy cotton squares and showed her how to mark the sewing line with a pencil and ruler.

The only other woman already present was Susan Gasset. She was small-boned and pretty, with short dark hair that curled appealingly around her face.

Edith White introduced her to Lily. "Susan works at the movie house in the evening. She sells the tickets."

Susan smiled and said, "And I make the popcorn, in case you ever wonder why my hair smells of stale butter. I've seen you at church. You live up at the top of the hill in one of the mansions, don't you?" There wasn't any resentment in her tone.

"I've never noticed that about your hair," Edith said, with unusual tact.

"That's why I keep it so short," Susan replied. "So I can wash it every morning. It's either popcorn or rabbit smell."

"Rabbit?" Lily asked.

Susan put down her squares of fabric for a moment. "My sister Bernadette lives with me and the children. She raises rabbits to eat and sells the fur when she can find a buyer. She takes care of my children while I work evenings. I share part of my salary with her, and she supplies us with rabbits to eat. I have, at last count, nineteen recipes for rabbit meat," she joked. "But none of them can disguise that it's rabbit."

Lily laughed. "Please don't let Mrs. Prinney know about this, or she'll raise rabbits too."

Susan smiled. "No, she buys them from my sister."

Lily noticed there was no mention of a husband on the scene. She knew better than to ask. "How many children do you have?" she inquired instead.

"Three. All under eight years old. They're in the kitchen with Edith's maid, who's giving them milk with bread-and-butter sandwiches. Bernadette is slaughtering rabbits this morning, and we never let the children know she does it." She said this quietly, so the children wouldn't hear her. "We just tell them that a few of the rabbits ran away to live in the woods."

Edith White had the women working and was supervising in the kitchen when Nina Pratt, the next member of the club, was shown into the sewing parlor by the maid. As Lily remembered, Phoebe said Nina was the town hairdresser. Nina's appearance surprised Lily. She was in her fifties. She looked tired. Her hands were red and chapped from the chemicals she used. Her own hair was thin, gray, and lank. And she was very quiet, introducing herself to Lily quite formally.

"Aren't your children with you today, Susan?" Nina said, subsiding with a small groan of relief in an armchair with a side table and good light.

"They're in the kitchen, eating bread and butter," Susan said, without taking her eyes from her work on some dark fabric with a pinstripe.

"Such quiet children," Nina said wearily, picking up a pile of colorful calico squares and looking them over. Lily learned later that Edith always gave her the prettiest fabric because

Nina was the best at putting colors together attractively.

The next arrival was Peggy Rismiller, the wife of the Episcopal minister in Voorburg. She, too, looked tired. She didn't pretend to be interested in sewing for the poor, but Lily had heard that their hostess—Mrs. White as Lily insisted on calling her properly in her own mind—was the most generous contributor to the church, and Peggy appeared to know where her social duties should be focused.

Edith emerged from the kitchen. "Peggy, dear—" she said.

"There were girls coming around the side of your house as I arrived," Peggy said.

"Those girl hoboes," Nina snapped. "They're always bothering us, as if we were any better off than they are."

"But you are," Susan said with a smile. "You have a job."

"They could get jobs too," Nina said angrily. "Most of the out-of-work men who come by for food insist on working for it. If it weren't for them, my shop would have fallen down a year ago. One of them told me the next time he was in town, he'd paint the porch for me if I would buy the paint and a brush and feed him."

Edith took over the conversation. "The girl hoboes would work if they had skills. They've been turned out of their homes because they were considered useless. We should pity them."

"Some of them might know how to sew," Susan said. "Do we want to invite them to work with us?" She was deliberately provoking Edith, but with an innocent-looking grin.

For once, Edith was disconcerted. "In my house? I think not."

The youngest member arrived before the discussion could continue. Ruby Heggan was only nineteen and brought along her infant, disappearing into the next room to nurse him when he became fretful. She was a tiny, pretty girl with lots of blond curly hair and had her baby wrapped in a lovely mixed-sherbet-colored blanket. She spoke up before anyone could introduce her to Lily.

"I'm pregnant again," she announced, on the brink of tears, to the Voorburg Ladies League.

Lily hoped the childless Edith would keep quiet and not congratulate Ruby. But her hopes were dashed. "You'll be glad someday to have children of your own," the hostess said. "I only had the orphaned niece of my first husband's sister. She lived with us until Bernard died."

Some of the rest of the women murmured sympathetically to Ruby, however. Most of them knew how hard and frightening it was to raise children in these bad times.

"Where's Roxanne?" Phoebe asked. "It's not like her to be late to a meeting."

"I saw her as I passed through the town," Ruby said, still sniffling. "She was carrying a bag into the greengrocer's."

"Is that Roxanne Anderson?" Lily asked. "Mrs. Prinney has mentioned her several times. She envies her her vegetable garden."

"It's quite impressive," Edith commented. "She works very hard on it, and so do her children and her brother, though her husband doesn't seem to get into the act. I never walk by the house without seeing someone weeding or watering. We'll wait for her before I tell you why I called you together."

Chapter 3

Roxanne Anderson came in a few minutes later, looking furious. "Those darned hobo girls! Sorry I'm late, but I was watching for them. They're stealing my vegetables when nobody's looking. I wanted to catch them at it and give them what for."

"We waited for you, Roxanne," Edith said repressively, and introduced Lily as the newest member of the group.

Lily had heard of Roxanne Anderson from Mrs. Prinney, and though they'd never met, Lily recognized her as someone she'd often seen in town as she carried baskets to the greengrocer with her long-striding walk and look of determination. Roxanne was a tall, strong woman with darker and straighter red hair than Phoebe's. Lily guessed she was in her late thirties or early forties. The fair skin on her face and arms was sunburned, and her nose, chin, and forehead were peeling. Her hands were clean but rough and cal-loused. She wore a somewhat faded checkered dress that strained across her shoulders, as if she'd developed muscles since she'd purchased it. But it was starched and neatly pressed.

"I'm so glad to meet you. The Prinneys live with us now, and Mrs. Prinney greatly admires your gardening," Lily said.

Roxanne smiled at this, displaying large white perfect teeth. "Mrs. Prinney's a good woman, but she won't listen to my advice about tomatoes. She waters them too much and will get bland re-sults. I'll get to tell her 'I told you so' by the end of summer. Edith, would you thread my needle? You know my near vision is going." She sat down with a stack of cut-up table linens and got out spectacles and a small box of embroidery thread.

"Roxanne's our artist," Susan Gasset said to Lily. "She embroiders flowers on the patches. Hers are the prettiest quilts."

Roxanne's face got even redder. "Go along," she said. "You just say that to get me to work. Let me tell you about those girls—"

Edith squelched her firmly again. "You may talk about it later, Roxanne. I called you together today to tell you good news."

It seemed that Edith had visited a second cousin in a town outside Philadelphia the week before, and the cousin took her to the "town truck." It was an old bus that had been converted to a shop, with the seats removed and shelves installed instead. It was a trading truck, which traveled around town and the surrounding countryside. The community had purchased the bus and paid the meager wages of the driver.

"A trading truck?" several women asked as Edith drew a quick breath.

"The people of the town trade goods in the truck," Edith said. "There was a man with fresh milk. You know, these days farmers are having to pour their milk out on the ground many places because they can't afford to ship it to cities."

"I saw that in the paper," Roxanne said, angry again. "So wasteful when many children are starved for milk. It's immoral."

Edith didn't want any more interruptions and stared fiercely at Roxanne. "If I may continue? The farmer doesn't get money at the town truck. He gets credit tokens called scrip for his milk. So much scrip for so many bottles of milk. And in turn he can buy things he needs from the truck with the scrip. No money ever changes hands."

"Scrip?" Susan Gasset asked.

"Think of scrip as written tokens," Edith said.

"Scrip?" Roxanne asked. "What's the value of the scrip?"

"That's what we need to decide," Edith White said. "Meat and milk would be more valuable than vegetables. Do you agree?" she asked, casting her eye around the group.

Phoebe spoke up. "I think it depends on how much meat or how many vegetables."

"Good point, my dear," Edith said cheerfully, apparently assuming she had everyone's agreement to the general plan.

"I like this!" Susan said. "My sister Bernadette's rabbits could be traded for beef—if anyone had beef."

Nina Pratt spoke up. "I don't grow any food. What good would it do me?"

Edith jumped on this. She seemed to be well prepared. "You have a skill, Nina. You could give a chit for a small amount of scrip, maybe one credit, for a good haircut and a bigger chit, three or four credits, for a permanent wave, and you wouldn't have to spend the money you make on those without scrip to buy food at the trading truck."

"I'm not sure I understand," Nina said.

"You'd write on pieces of stiff paper, ONE UNIT OF SCRIP TO NINA'S HAIR PARLOR. GOOD FOR A CUT. That's what you'd give as your benefit. Someone else would 'buy' the scrip for—oh, let's say," Edith said, as naughty as a sixteen-year-old girl, "six rolls of good lavatory paper, which you could buy with the returned scrip. It would be like trading a haircut for the lavatory paper, but you wouldn't have to bargain with the customer."

"Would everyone set their own scrip price?" Roxanne asked suspiciously.

Edith hadn't considered this. "I guess we'll have to talk about that."

Roxanne was determined to have an answer. "A dozen of my carrots is worth more than a dozen of anyone else's. They're straighter and fatter and never woody. I went to a lot of trouble getting river sand to grow them in. Who would decide?"

Ruby hadn't said anything yet. Now she spoke up. "Wait. What if Roxanne priced her carrots too high and they sat around drying out in the truck for two weeks and nobody wanted or could afford them? She's gotten her scrip and nobody got the carrots."

This stymied everyone: not only the question but the fact that Ruby had asked it.

Niggling conversations, a few of them slightly heated, broke out. This was the sort of disorganized discussion Edith White couldn't tolerate.

"That's what we're here to decide," she said, in almost a shout. "I propose that we set prices in scrip for everything we can think of, no matter the quality. Just specify the number of items."

"First we'd need a truck," Phoebe put in, trying to throw a verbal bucket of cold water on the sizzling tone of the conversation.

"I can find someone to donate the truck," Edith said sharply. Lily suspected Edith didn't grasp that Phoebe was trying to help out by changing the course of the discussion.

"And who drives the truck and buys the gas and decides where to drive it?" Mrs. Rismiller asked. She was the only one referred to by everybody but Edith by her married name, being the wife of a minister. "And what is he paid?"

Phoebe asked, "Why should it be a *he* who is paid?"

Edith looked up at the ceiling for a moment. "Because so many men are out of work, my dear."

"And many of their wives and daughters are working instead," Phoebe persisted. "Everything we've talked about so far is domestic. Food and clothing. Most men have no concept of the relative worth of these items. I think the driver ought to be a woman. Lots of women know how to drive these days. And they know the value of household objects." Phoebe suddenly stopped and blushed at giving such a strong, long speech.

Edith White didn't come back with a direct reply. "I'll tell you all that this worked where my cousin lives. I'll write her and ask your questions and concerns. I might even telephone her. We'll meet again when I receive the answers. Now let's get back to our sewing."

Lily felt badly about the way the proposal had gone. Mrs. White had obviously expected full agreement, but she hadn't done her homework. Lily, who spent a great deal of her own time toting up numbers, had no idea how it could work.

Someone clumped down the stairs. Henry White came into the room. "A little hen's nest of gossip, eh?" he said with a grin.

Edith smiled back. "You know better, dear.

We're plotting a new way of helping the people of Voorburg."

"Ah," Henry said, putting a hand on Edith's shoulder. He was a tall, fair, handsome man and looked a bit younger than his wife. Lily was surprised that Edith leaned a bit to touch her cheek to his hand. Edith's smile was a little crooked, she realized, as if one side of her mouth didn't work quite the way the other side did.

"I wouldn't want to interrupt anything so worthwhile," Henry said, with a toothy smile. "I'll just go in the kitchen and sit with the children. I've always liked bread-and-butter sandwiches."

Edith turned to watch him for a moment as he walked away with a friendly wave to the women.

"I don't know what came over me to speak that way," Phoebe said, as they were leaving an hour later, her face flushing again. Lily had errands in town and was going toward Phoebe's hat shop anyway.

"You asked good questions," Lily said. "We need to know more about how this is to work before we get involved and try to fix mistakes as they happen. I noticed that Edith has an oddly uneven smile. And she slightly favors her left arm as if it hurts a bit. Has she had a stroke or something? She seems too young for that."

"She was probably in some sort of accident in her youth," Phoebe said.

Lily heard someone coming up quickly behind them and turned. It was Roxanne Anderson. "I'm glad you spoke up, Miss Twinkle," she said, when she caught up to them. At least she was observing Edith White's rule that first names were used only at meetings. "Mrs. White means well, but she sometimes goes off like a firecracker without thinking where she'll land."

"I think she knew it," Lily said. "It must have hurt her pride to admit she needed more information."

Roxanne laughed. "She only admitted that *we* needed more information. Miss Brewster, I'm glad you joined the group. I've been trying to get Emmaline Prinney to come along, but she says she's too busy taking care of Grace and Favor."

"It's the truth, I'm afraid," Lily said with a smile. "I hardly ever see her even sit down except at meals."

Roxanne went back to her original subject and addressed Phoebe again. "Mrs. White has a good husband who has a job. She's got money and free time. I don't hold that against her. I used to have that kind of life, and I wouldn't have willingly given it up. But she can't understand what some of the rest of us are going through."

She turned to Lily.

"My husband had a job selling farm tools. The company went bankrupt. He gets dressed in a suit and tie every day and goes out looking for another job. It's very hard for us. He was such a

nice man, a good daddy, always telling jokes and
tickling the kids. And now he's so grouchy and
angry, the children hide from him in the evenings.
This is the sort of life Edith might hear about but
never understand."

She suddenly looked embarrassed at having re-
vealed so much about her family.

"Now I must be off. I want to catch those hobo
girls before they discover what's under the turnip
foliage and steal those as well."

Phoebe and Lily trudged along, dispirited by
what Roxanne had said. "I never thought I'd say
this," Lily said quietly, "but right now I'm glad I
don't have an out-of-work husband and sad,
frightened children."

"Me too," Phoebe admitted. "It's hard enough
to keep my own spirits up most of the time without being responsible for propping up a whole
family."

"Tell me a little about Ruby," Lily said. "She
looks very young to be having a second baby."

"I don't know her well," Phoebe said, "but I
know the family she married into. They've been
around here forever. They had a big house, and a
lot of land and grew hops for the breweries, so Pro-
hibition destroyed them before the rest of us. They
started growing corn and wheat, but they aren't
much good at it. There are five boys. Ruby married
the youngest one. The older ones aren't married—
for good reason; no one would have them. Ruby
and her husband can't afford a house of their own,

so they live with his tartar of a mother, his father, and the other four boys in a tiny house the Heggans had to move to when they sold the big one."

"How awful for her," Lily said.

"Louis, Ruby's husband, seems to be a nice enough boy, but the others are big-mouthed drunken louts. They're always in trouble. They almost burned down Mabel's Cafe last year. Claimed they couldn't remember what inspired them."

"Poor Ruby. And another baby on the way."

Phoebe blushed again and said, "I don't know how they managed it in that household."

Lily laughed. "I wonder about that too."

"The last time we met, Ruby told us that Louis was talking about borrowing money from someone and getting an old car to go to California. He thinks everybody's all right out there."

Lily frowned. "An old car. Across the whole country. With an infant and another on the way. I'd be terrified."

"Ruby is. But maybe the news about the new baby on the way will make Louis cool his heels."

"Or take off on his own," Lily said, without even thinking.

"I think that might be what really scares Ruby," Phoebe replied. "So many men have just disappeared when things got too bad. And they call *us* the weaker sex."

Chapter 4

Lily and Phoebe chatted until they got to Phoebe's hat shop, then Lily took a look at the butcher's for Mrs. Prinney, who hoped against hope there would be a pork roast going begging. There wasn't one. Putting off the long trudge back up the hill, Lily stopped in at Jack Summer's office.

Jack was the brash young editor who'd been selected to replace the former editor at Lily and Robert's urging. Jack knew their Great-uncle Horatio had owned the paper and assumed Lily and Robert were now the owners. Few people knew the truth.

Great-uncle Horatio had made their inheritance of his many businesses, the property, gold, cash, flamboyant Duesenberg Model J Derham Tourster that Robert so loved, and even the mansion Lily and Robert lived in, conditional on their staying there for ten years and earning their own living. That was why they had re-named the place Grace and Favor, after the benefices of old. Lily and Robert had been spoiled society brats when their father lost his fortune and committed suicide, leaving his children with practically nothing but eight hundred dollars and their mother's pier glass, two trunks, and a suit-case apiece for their personal belongings—mainly clothing, letters, and mementos—and no commercial skills at all.

Mr. Prinney, the executor of the estate, had the onerous job of seeing to it that they fulfilled the conditions of the will, which was one of the rea-sons he and his wife had moved into the mansion with them. He acted as their jailer, boarder, ad-viser, and attorney and had gradually become a friend to them as well.

Lately, Lily wondered if keeping this a secret had been a good idea. At first both brother and sister had been embarrassed by the restriction. It showed them up as formerly useless orna-ments with no talents other than social ones. But as almost a year passed, they'd both started changing.

Robert made himself useful around the man-sion. He'd even persuaded Mr. Prinney that he could use a few common tools if Mr. Prinney would authorize the purchase.

Lily spent a lot of time learning about the es-tate's holdings and had impressed the lawyer with her grasp of business and the thrift she'd learned after two dreary years of utter poverty.

But on the other hand, keeping their true situation private set them apart from the villagers they would have to live with. Many of the Voorburgians considered the pair as rich and as useless as Uncle Horatio had known them to be before the Crash.

Jack Summer was pacing the newspaper office when Lily strolled in.

"Just the person I was thinking about!" he said. "I want to cover the Bonus Army March in Washington. Several of Voorburg's veterans are there, and I think they should be interviewed. I've already got enough material for next Monday's paper and I'd only go for a few days."

Lily sat down, wishing it were ladylike to take her shoes off and put her feet up on a chair to refresh them for the journey up the hill. "What do you mean? You've been covering it since it started."

"Sure I have, but it's all secondhand. I haven't learned anything from anyone who's actually in the march, only other reporters who are covering it and what I hear on the radio. I want to go down there and talk to real people. Especially the ones from here."

Lily hesitated. She read every issue before it was published. Mr. Prinney still feared that, without supervision, Jack might go off the rails and print something to bring the paper down in flames.

"One thing you haven't really touched on since the very beginning is how and why the march is taking place," Lily said.

"I tried to explain that when I first sniffed out the story, back when Congress started hearings on the Patman bill, which was disputed as long ago as 1929. Stubbins wouldn't print it. You know what a cream puff he was about anything upsetting."

"But that was years ago. A lot of people will have forgotten the details and background, even if they were told about it." She didn't identify herself as one of them, although she was.

"You know from what your last guest at Grace and Favor said about the Great War and how horrible it was."

"Of course I do. But you and I were children when it was fought."

Jack sighed. "That's not the point. The original bonus bill was passed in 1924 and was to pay every American veteran of the Great War."

"How much?" Lily asked.

"A dollar and a quarter a day for those who served on the field of battle, a dollar a day for those who served here."

"That's a lot of money," Lily said.

"It is. And it was supposed to earn interest as well—when it was paid out. Which wasn't supposed to be until 1945."

Lily couldn't disguise her ignorance and surprise. "Nineteen forty-five? Twenty-one years later?"

Jack leaned back in his chair, looking smug at her reaction. "It was criminal to hold it back that long. Mind you, this was five years before the Crash and nobody knew it was coming. Most of the men who hadn't been gassed or seriously injured had gone back to work. Maybe the point was to give them money for retirement." Jack shrugged. "Now most of those veterans who are still alive are out of work and desperate for what's owed them. They're willing to forgo the rest of the interest."

"How much would it be per person now?"

"About a thousand smackeroos. More than many of them would make if they were employed."

"This is what you need to say again, Jack," Lily said emphatically. "It's high time people knew."

"I knew it then. But I wasn't allowed to say it, Lily. Remember, I was a new reporter then, with a boss who didn't want to rock the boat."

"So say it now. I know I'm not the only one who is badly informed," Lily exclaimed.

"But I want to say it for the men of Voorburg who are camped in Washington, D.C. That's why I want to go there. To get firsthand accounts of what they're suffering to get what the government promised them."

"You'll have to speak to Mr. Prinney about that.

Who would pay for the train and hotel and your food?"

"The newspaper, of course. You know how little I'm paid."

"You better let me pave the way. You know what a penny-pincher he is."

"But it's up to you and Robert, isn't it?"

Lily knew she sounded prim when she said, "He knows much more than we do about the newspaper budget. We trust his opinion." *We have to*, she thought of saying, but bit back the words.

"Still, I like the idea of your going," she went on. "Firsthand information about people the town knows is best. And I can present it more tactfully to Mr. Prinney than you can. You'd get all hot under the collar if he argued with you. I'm on my way there now; he's working at home today. I'll try to talk him round."

Jack didn't like this, but he had to agree. "Give me a ring-a-ding here when you're done."

Lily hated it when he used slang. He had such a good grasp of perfect grammar. But this was not the time to mention it. She turned coy. "I have to walk clear up the hill. It would hurry things up if you gave me a lift and hid the motorcycle until I signal."

Jack laughed. "You once said you'd rather walk anywhere than ride in the sidecar."

"A girl can change her mind, can't she?" she said sweetly.

*   *   *

By the time they had sped up the hill, Lily felt as if half her hair had been ripped out in the wind. She must look a wreck. She tried to step gracefully from the sidecar and nearly fell out, which just made it worse. Jack parked by the gatehouse, but he couldn't help but hear what Robert called to her as she headed for the mansion.

"Lily, guess what we found in the old icehouse."

"A million dollars?" Lily asked.

"Nope. Guess again."

"Oh, Robert. You know I'll never guess."

"A body."

"Hmm. A body of what? A possum? A fox?"

"Lily, you're so unimaginative. The body of a man."

Lily hugged herself as if protecting herself from the news. "A man? Who? Haven't we already had enough deaths here?"

"This isn't a recent one. It's more like a mummy."

"An old Indian or something?"

"Not quite. A very well-dressed gentleman."

Jack had quietly approached, and startled Lily when he said, "Where is he?"

"Already on his way to Albany," Robert said.

"Whew," Jack said. "I was afraid Doc Polhemus would be involved. He's such a fool and a gossip." Jack was one of the people young Dr. Polhemus often brought up by name when he blathered about his wart theory, claiming he'd cured Jack and others of warts by identifying and destroying what he called the "mother" wart. It made Jack mad to have this secret shared in public.

"We all know that," Robert said. "Chief Walker took care that Dr. Polhemus didn't know about it until he'd contacted the coroner up there. Polhemus is out of town for a couple of days and a brand-new doctor from Fishkill is filling in for him. Walker told the substitute the man could have been from anywhere. Not necessarily local. Walker asked the State of New York to step in."

"Lily," Jack said, "don't you have something to do?"

"What?" she asked, still trying to absorb the bad news.

"The Bonus March," Jack said. "Remember?"

"Oh, yes." Lily hurried inside.

"Do you really have no idea whose body it is?" Jack asked, when Lily was apparently out of hearing range.

"I've only lived here for a short time. And this guy's been dead for a long time," Robert replied.

"Oh, wasn't he just a skeleton in clothing?"

"No, I told you he was like a mummy. I guess because the old icehouse was so sturdy and well chinked." Robert thought for a moment. "Maybe he was put in there in very cold, dry weather and froze solid."

"Couldn't anyone else identify him?"

"There were only the Harbinger brothers helping me take down the icehouse. And—" Robert
paused, trying to think of a tactful way to explain.

"And what?" Jack demanded.

"His face is unrecognizable. Hands as well. The
parts of him that were exposed. Mice probably."

Jack turned a little bit green. "I see. Did
Howard Walker have any guess how long he'd
been there?"

"Nope. I don't know how anyone could tell. If
Great-uncle Horatio was still using the icehouse,
the body probably wasn't put there until after he
died. Or maybe not. Grace and Favor stood vacant for quite a while after Great-uncle Horatio
died."

"But was it still in use when he was alive?
When was the ice storage shed added to the side
of the pantry?"

Robert scratched his head. "Again, it was here
when we arrived. Might have been put on years
or even decades ago."

"Who would know?" Jack nagged.

"I have no idea. Great-uncle Horatio's dead.
His staff, which was small, all came with him
when his Aunt Flora died. I assume they all went
back to wherever they came from. There wasn't
anyone around but hoboes when we came here,
and they all lived in the kitchen."

"So there isn't anyone who would remember?"

"Probably not. Why do you care so much about
dates?" Robert asked.

"Well, obviously it's local news and I'm the editor of the paper. But how long the body could have been there would be a clue as to who it might be. If, for example, the new icehouse was built onto the pantry in 1920, the body could have been put in the old one in the woods anytime after that. So you'd have a long list of men it might be. If it was much later, you cut down on the possibilities."

"Hmm. I hadn't thought of it that way. Are you going to investigate the murder?"

"Murder? You didn't say it was a murder!" Jack exclaimed.

Robert ran his hands through his normally well-groomed hair in frustration. "I figure it had to be. He was bashed on the back of the head and laid out very formally with his hands on his chest, tied lightly together with some sort of string. I don't think you could consider it suicide or a natural death."

"You should have said earlier." Jack was angry. "Of course it must be investigated. But I brought Lily up here to see if you and she will pay to send me to Washington to cover our Voorburg men in the Bonus March. I don't guess Albany will know anything until I get back. If I'm allowed to go on your nickel. Today is Friday. I want to leave tomorrow and be back by Wednesday."

"Who's putting together the newspaper in the meantime?" Robert asked.

"I've already got it done and ready for printing."

"You'll be busy putting together the next issue when you get back. I guess it's up to me to play detective," Robert said.

He rubbed his hands together in anticipation. It would make Jack nearly insane to think about losing his story.

Chapter 5

Lily didn't go see Mr. Prinney right away. She'd lurked just inside the front door trying unsuccessfully to eavesdrop until Jack Summer reluctantly left, saying to Robert, "Let me know what Mr. Prinney says about me going to Washington."

"Somebody's got to tell Mr. Prinney about the body in the icehouse," Lily said, when Robert came inside too quickly and found her eavesdropping.

"I told him," Robert said. "He's not very happy about it."

"Nor am I!" Lily exclaimed. "The last thing we need is another dead body. Grace and Favor already has a bad reputation for people dying here."

"Every old house has had people die in them," Robert said.

"Of natural causes," Lily said. "Not all who died here qualify. I've got to talk to Mr. Prinney about Jack's interviewing the Bonus Marchers."

"Do. And tell Prinney it's a good idea," Robert said.

"You think so?"

"It gives me some leeway," Robert said mysteriously. Normally she'd have questioned such a remark, but she had other things on her mind. She merely shrugged and went to Mr. Prinney's office off the front entry hall.

When she'd put Jack's proposal to the elderly lawyer, she added, "I think it's a good idea. Local interest in national affairs. And Robert agrees with me."

Anything that would cost the estate money, however little, came under the elderly gentleman's purview. "I'd have to know exactly what it will cost and what we'd benefit from the investment."

"Jack can explain the cost," Lily said. "As for the benefits, it's national news with a strong local interest. He told me at least five veterans from Voorburg are at the encampment, and at least two of them have their whole families along. I think it would increase circulation if he interviewed people known to Voorburg instead of simply writing about something that's going on a long way from us."

"I take your point," Mr. Prinney said reluctantly. "Get a budget from Jack Summer. But have

Robert run you down the hill. I'm waiting for an important call."

Lily hunted down Robert, who was, not surprisingly, polishing up the Duesie. "Mr. Prinney agreed," she said, "subject to setting a financial limit to Jack's trip. But the phone is tied up. I think one of the Prinneys' daughters is having a baby any day now. Or maybe he's waiting to learn something about the body in the old icehouse. Drive me to town, would you?"

"Don't you want to hear about the man we found? Or did you manage to overhear my conversation with Jack?"

"No, you both were speaking very quietly. I just can't manage two things at once."

Robert dropped her off at the newspaper office and went to run some other errands. "I'll be parked down near the river. Come find me when you're ready to go home."

Lily found Jack Summer in his tiny office, feet on the desk, smoking a cheap cigar and reading a newspaper someone sent him from California.

"At least open a window, would you?" Lily said, waving at the cloud of smoke.

"Does Mr. Prinney agree I should go to Washington?" Jack said, struggling with a window that had to be propped open with a stick.

"Only if you tell us exactly what it'll cost."

Jack sat back down, grinding out the cigar with a look of distaste. He opened a drawer in the desk and pulled out a scrap of paper and handed it

over. He'd listed round-trip railway fares via
New York and on to Washington. A food al-
lowance. And he'd allowed for the possibility of
having to stay in an inexpensive hotel for one
night.

"Why the hotel? Aren't you going to stay with
the men you're interviewing?" Lily asked.

"If they have a place for me to bed down, I
will. But they're not exactly expecting company,
and I'll arrive late in the day. I'm not sleeping
on the Washington sidewalk, even for a good
story."

Lily folded the paper and put it in her bag.
"This looks reasonable to me. The more I think
about it, the better I like the idea."

She left the office, with Jack sadly contemplat-
ing the cigar as if wondering if it was worthwhile
to relight it, and set out to find Robert. While she
was walking through town, she saw Edith White
and her husband getting out of their automobile.
Henry went around and gallantly took her hand
to help her out. As they walked arm in arm down
the block like newlyweds, Lily noticed that Edith
had a very slight limp to her walk. Whatever accident or ailment Edith might have had could ac-
count for why she appeared older than her
handsome husband.

As Lily was standing watching the couple, the
greengrocer called out from the door of his shop.
"Could I have a word with you, Miss Brewster?"

"Certainly, Mr. Bradley," Lily said.

He gestured toward a bench at the front of the shop. When Lily was seated, he cleared his throat and said, "I hear that Mrs. Prinney is growing her own vegetables. Why is that?"

The question took Lily by surprise. "We don't know either."

Mr. Bradley took a deep, regretful breath. "Seems to me, Miss Brewster—begging your pardon if I'm speaking out of turn—that we're all in this mess together. You rich folks up the hill rightly ought to keep buying from the townspeople, or there may not *be* townspeople for long. We'll all be on the dole. If the dole lasts."

Lily was shocked. This was one of the mildest, most polite men in Voorburg. He must be genuinely upset to speak to her this way but simply had to say his peace.

"Mr. Bradley, I'll talk with Mrs. Prinney about this. Today."

"Thanks, Miss Brewster." Blushing furiously at his outspoken remarks, he almost fled into the safety of his shop.

Lily sat on the bench for a few minutes more, truly stunned by what he'd said. She realized how hard it had been for him to speak up—and what's more, from his viewpoint he was right. But how could she tell Mrs. Prinney that all the older woman's hard work had been unpatriotic?

Lily wasn't normally upset by confrontations, but this one had come out of the blue and she was shaken. She started to get up, but her knees wobbled.

As she perched on the bench, waiting until she was calmer, she was vaguely aware of people passing by. An effeminate young man carrying a stuffed rucksack and a battered violin case, his eyes cast down, was hurrying along as if late for an appointment.

A middle-aged man who seemed faintly familiar came along next, but she didn't remember his name. He wore a shabby suit, carried a flattish canvas-and-leather case, and walked briskly, glancing about furtively.

A young woman down the street near Mabel's Cafe, wearing what was once a nice red dress but was much too tight on her voluptuous figure, was lounging at the corner of the building, trying to light a cigarette.

A well-dressed woman driving a car with Vermont plates went into Phoebe Twinkle's shop. Lily hoped Phoebe would sell her several of her most stylish hats.

Lily finally got up, knees still shaking slightly, and went to find Robert. The spotless butter-yellow Duesie was parked in front of the small house Chief of Police Howard Walker currently occupied, with the front room serving as his office. She was surprised that he apparently was still living here. It was so close to the river and the train tracks that it must be hard to sleep between the deafening sounds of the trains. Not to mention that the house actually sat a little lower than the tracks and often flooded when there were heavy rains. It was a bad place to have to live and work.

The two men had seen her approach, and Walker opened the door to her as she raised her hand to knock. "Come in, Miss Brewster. Robert and I are having a cold beer. Would you like one?"

"Anything cold sounds good to me," she said, fanning herself with her small flat handbag. "It's getting awfully hot, and the heat makes the river stink. How do you stand living here?"

"I won't have to for much longer," Walker said. "Jack Summer and his cousin Ralph Summer, my deputy, are moving to a house that's been abandoned, and I'm getting their adjoining rooms in the boardinghouse next week. The place smells of old cabbage, but at least it's farther up the hill and is shaded by trees."

He brought her a glass of beer and turned the creaking electric fan so she'd get more of the air. Lily sat down in a straight chair at the table and took a long, cold drink before saying, "So whose body did Robert find?"

Both men shrugged. "Nobody knows," Robert said, "but Chief Walker's been on the phone to Albany. There was a label in the mummy's suit with the name of a tailor in New York City. We're going to run down there tomorrow and see if they can match the measurements to anyone. What's the name of the place again?"

Walker said, "I've got it written down somewhere. Blackstone's of Fifth Avenue, I think."

"Why is this your first thing to check?" Lily
asked. "Can't anybody around here recognize
him?"

The men exchanged a glance. Robert was the
first to speak. "I guess you're not a good eaves-
dropper after all, Lily. He's pretty well pre-
served. The icehouse must have been almost
airtight and he's more or less a mummy—except
for his face and hands." Robert paused for a moment but went on before she could ask. "There
were apparently animals in there who did a bit of
nibbling."

Lily gasped, hugged herself, and said, "I wish
you hadn't told me that."

"You asked," Robert said.

Lily drew a deep breath and took another sip of
her beer, which was already warming up. "Have
you any idea how long he'd been there? Or if he
was local? Did he have any identification, maybe
a suitcase or wallet? Maybe he was just passing
through and we'll never know who he was."

Her voice was nearly drowned out by a fast
freight train approaching and blowing its whistle
deafeningly.

"Nothing else," Howard Walker shouted over
the noise. He put up a hand to signal that he'd
finish when the train had passed. "Someone had
bashed him in the back of the head, and if he had
anything with him to say who he was, it's proba-

bly washed down the river into the Atlantic long ago," he said, when the train was gone. "But they or he or she must have missed the label in his suit. It's all we've got to go on."

"Did he have teeth?" Lily asked.

"Yes," Walker said. "Good dental work, the guy in Albany says. But until we have some idea of where he came from, and unless we get information on his clothing, there's no way to know who did the work or where they live."

"We'll take the suit to the city tomorrow," Robert said, "if we can borrow the suit today from the forensic guy in Albany."

"Tomorrow's Saturday," Walker said. "Will the shop be open?"

"I suppose so," Robert said. "Most men who can afford to buy a suit these days probably only have Saturday afternoons and Sundays off."

"I'm not sure this is worth the trouble," Walker said. "The guy in Albany doesn't believe that he was even in the icehouse for very long. He said mummification takes a year-round hot, dry, windy climate. Like deserts. That certainly doesn't describe the Hudson River Valley."

Robert said, "But if he was put in the icehouse during such a spell in the summer it could be. The icehouse was the tightest-built structure I've ever come across. It had to be, to keep the ice cold all summer. Or even if he was put there in the coldest, driest part of a very frigid winter long after it was used for storing ice, the same might apply. I can't imagine someone moved him in that condition from some desert. His body would have been too fragile to move and keep intact."

"And besides, you want to go to the city," Walker said. "And so do I."

Chapter 6

As Lily and Robert were driving up the hill to Grace and Favor, Robert asked, "What's really on your mind, Toots? You don't seem to have much interest in the icehouse discovery." He slowed the huge automobile to reach around front and brush a squashed bug off the windshield.

"A conversation with Mr. Bradley," she said.

"The greengrocer? Is that all?" Robert laughed. "How could that be more interesting than a dead body almost on our doorstep?"

"It's more immediate, for one thing." Lily recounted the conversation she'd had with Bradley as she passed his shop. "Robert, he was right."

Robert had stopped laughing.

"I don't know how to bring this up to Mrs. Prinney, or if I even should," Lily said. "I told him I would. I guess I have to live up to my promise."

"They're both afraid," Robert said. "Bradley's afraid of his business going under if people grow

their own vegetables. Mrs. Prinney's afraid his
business will fail and we won't have anything to
eat. It's a self-fulfilling prophecy if too many people feel that way. We're all afraid down deep inside. I think it hits men harder."

Robert, a born and raised bon vivant, had frequently said surprisingly wise things since 1929,
when brother and sister were forced to get to
know each other instead of merely passing
through the same homes, sharing the same parents, and meeting mostly at parties. She wondered if he'd always been this perceptive, and just
never had to use his brains and heart. Perhaps the
trait had lain dormant for most of his life.

"Including you?" Lily asked.

"Nope, not me," Robert said.

He got out and opened the garage and came
back and moved the enormous butter-yellow automobile inside. When the Duesie was safely put
away, he said, "Let's go look at the river."

Instead of going inside, they went to what Lily
thought of as the "viewing bench" under a tree,
where she often sat and brushed Agatha, her per-
petually shedding adopted dog, while she con-
templated the water traffic passing below. What
was inside those barges being pushed along by
tugs? Where had they come from? Where were
they going?

When they were comfortably seated, Robert
went on as if there hadn't been a break in the conversation. "I never considered when we were

growing up that I'd have to get a job in order to provide heat, food, or a home for a wife and children. I thought I'd wait for the right woman, as rich as we once were, and go right on living the same kind of life our parents did—traveling, dabbling in investments, playing polo, drinking too much, going to parties, wearing outrageously priced clothing.

"Instead," he went on, "I spent the early morning today preparing to tear down a shed in the woods and thinking what great wood it was and what I might be able to do with it. Bookshelves for my bedroom. Another bench like this one."

Lily looked askance. She had no idea he thought he knew how to do either of these projects.

"Of course, I won't take the wood," Robert went on. "It would look selfish and greedy to the Harbinger boys for what they think is a rich man, who obviously doesn't know how to build a thing, to grab it for himself. The boys will make better use of it than I ever could. Maybe sell it to buy food for their family or make a nice piece of furniture for their mother."

"I have the same problem with Jack Summer," Lily admitted. "He thinks we own the newspaper. He supposes we're dopes for always having to consult with Mr. Prinney over newspaper decisions. That we're wealthy idiots who can't make a simple decision for ourselves."

"And imagine what the townspeople had to

say about our guests last April when we made them pay to stay at Grace and Favor."

"Do you think people knew they were paying guests?" Lily asked.

Robert looked at her for a long moment with astonishment. "Did you suppose they didn't? Lily, gossip is the constant staple of a small town, even if the catastrophes we had here hadn't been reported in papers across the world. Or at least this country. I'll bet some of the locals are still chewing it over and criticizing us for being such greedy gerties."

"We made a mistake right up front, didn't we?" Lily said. This revelation had been forcing itself on her ever since the greengrocer spoke to her. How could she have been so dim? "We've been pretending since we came here that we really own the house and Uncle Horatio's assets, haven't we? We should have thought it out."

"We didn't know that," Robert reminded her. "We were both feeling sorry for ourselves for proving conclusively how absolutely useless we were without Dad's fortune. We were embarrassed at suddenly being poor. And we were frightened and humiliated by our failures already, like almost everyone is now."

"But why's it taken us so long to figure it out?" Lily asked.

"Because we had no idea this whole country was ever going to be in such terrible trouble, I suppose. Americans—even us when we were rich kids—believe, however theoretically, in work. Work hard and prosper and all that. We mistakenly thought we were personally above that once, but no longer. But when Americans—men in particular—can't get work at all, or see their life's assets disappear, they think it's somehow their fault."

"But it isn't. Not often."

"But they fear it is. Fear's at the heart of everything that's happening to this country. Men who see their children getting thinner and thinner, eating wild greens instead of meat, feel guilty. And feeling guilty makes them angry. And when a person is always angry at himself, he's angry with everyone. And especially the government that's letting it happen. In fact, President Hoover still denies that anything's wrong. He's a rich man himself and probably genuinely thinks everything would be hunky-dory if everyone just pulled themselves up by the bootstraps and acted happy with their lot. He only got into office because he was in charge of feeding the Europeans at America's expense after the Great War and did a good job. But he seems to think Americans should do it without any government help."

Agatha suddenly discovered they were back and tore toward the bench, barking hysterically.

"It shouldn't be that way," Lily said, petting the dog and shushing her.

"But it is. Remember how angry you always were when we lived in the fifth-floor cold-water tenement, both of us working the soles of our shoes off for peanuts and falling further and further behind?"

"I don't remember being angry," Lily responded. "I was just always tired to the bone. But I must have been wasting a lot of energy being furious at what had happened to us. I blamed Dad, I'm sorry to say. As if he'd lost his money and his life to spite us. How stupid of me. Agatha, don't go from barking to whining," Lily said, lifting the dog up to sit between them.

"Dad wasn't thinking of us at all." There was a flash of real and rare anger in his voice. "Dad was thinking only of himself. Knowing then what we soon learned about ourselves, that he had no skills other than in living the good life—without having to make any effort. He just realized it before we did."

"But we didn't throw ourselves out a window and end it all," Lily argued.

"You can't tell me there weren't times before we came here that you didn't consider it," Robert said.

Lily smiled sadly. "I did, but I was too vain to imagine myself sprawled on a sidewalk, with my skirt up around my waist and my knickers showing. I imagined people gawking at me and saying, 'She should have mended them before she jumped.' "

Robert nearly fell off the bench laughing at this. "Only a woman would think that way," he said.

"Women are so much more practical than men. And frankly stronger in their minds. Look at Mrs. Gasset. The one whose husband did a bolt. She just keeps on going, taking care of her kids, being pleasant to the customers, working nights at the movie house. He, like most men, couldn't handle being out of work and ran off."

Lily said, "How can a woman with little children run off?" She had grown up with girls who were taught that they were to be ornamental, not strong-minded. But she herself had learned that being sweet and compliant and well dressed didn't count for much.

As they walked back to the mansion, Agatha circling around them hysterically, Lily asked, "So what are we going to do about telling the truth about our situation?"

"First, we're going to think about it for a while—this time," Robert said. "It'll be awkward for us no matter what. But we'll be safer."

"Safer? What does that mean?"

"I'm thinking about Reds."

"Oh, Robert, how silly."

"Not as silly as you think. The Communist Party is made up of the angriest people of all. And it's getting a foothold."

Lily wasn't convinced. "I knew a couple of girls at school who claimed to be Communists, and they were nutty. Everybody laughed at them. They fancied themselves as snotty intellectuals. They always dressed in black, baggy clothes."

"That's how it used to be, Lily. Not anymore. The party is growing. Haven't you noticed how many more men are gathering in Mabel's back room in their not very secret meetings?"

"Do you mean that?"

"I do. Communism is loony and dangerous. 'From each according to his ability, to each according to his need,' " he quoted. "It's an invitation to steal from competent hard workers and encourage the unskilled slackers. I can say this because I'm one of the unskilled slackers myself. It's wrong."

"Who are these new people who are joining?"

"The most angry ones," Robert said. "Deservedly angry, I'll admit, but desperately looking for any solution that might benefit them. Lots of farmers, for one thing. Old-line Republicans like we were, swinging entirely in the opposite direction. And no doubt lots of the folks in Detroit after the disgusting River Rouge massacre."

Lily looked perplexed.

"Don't you ever read any paper other than the *Voorburg-on-Hudson Times*?" Robert asked. "Henry Ford, that godlike person, lowered wages, extended the work hours, and speeded up the production lines," he explained. "Men were literally falling asleep on the line and going to work when they were sick, just to keep their jobs. Many of them were being injured. The workers and their families staged a peaceful march a few months ago in freezing temperatures, asking Ford to be rea-

sonable and fair. Ford's goons and the police
turned fire hoses and guns on them. Killed a couple outright. Some of the men in the march, as well
as the women and children, died later of pneumonia."

"I'm ashamed to say I didn't know about that.
I've had my nose too far into the bookkeeping,"
Lily admitted. "I had no idea. How horrible."

"You can bet the Commies got a lot of members
out of it," Robert said.

"But still," Lily said, "there can't be very many
of them."

"Victories don't always go to the powerful,
Lily. Fanaticism of the few can prevail. Look what
happened to the Tzar of Russia, with all his
armies. The fanatics executed him and his family
and took over. All it takes is the right leader at the
right time."

"Are you telling me the rich are in danger?
Even those, like us, who only *used* to be
wealthy?"

Robert considered. "I don't know. I hope I'm
wrong and would like to believe it, but I wouldn't
want to be part of Henry Ford's family right now.
Lily, we're living a stupid lie we started out of
sheer false pride. We seem like minor American
nobility to Voorburg—living in this monster of a
mansion and driving a Duesenberg. Look what
happened to even the minor nobility of Russia.
The few who weren't murdered fled to other Eu-
ropean countries and America and Canada with

only the clothes on their backs and maybe a jewel or two sewn into their underwear."

In spite of the heat of the summer day, Lily shivered.

"Do I tell Mrs. Prinney what the greengrocer said?" she asked quietly, as they got closer to the mansion.

Robert shrugged. "He should have tackled her himself, but since he's accused her—and us—of trying to ruin him, I think she should know."

"I was afraid that's what you'd say."

Chapter 7

Jack could have taken the train that left Voorburg at 9:07 A.M. and gone clear to Washington, D.C. But without consulting anyone, he left on the 6:38 train to see a bit of New York City along the way. The earlier train didn't make as many stops. Nor did it incur extra expense for anyone.

He hadn't been to the city for years. And the last time he went he was looking for a newspaper job and came back to Voorburg without joy. Only one underling would even see him personally, to tell him his chances were nil. This time he wasn't looking for a job. He just wanted to see the city. He'd talked the Brewsters into footing the bill to subscribe to several city papers and had new things simply to look at.

He arrived at what would have normally been the beginning of the morning rush hour, if it hadn't been a Saturday, and checked his suitcase. The first thing he noticed was that the streets were strangely empty of apple sellers. He'd heard so much about them crowding the sidewalks peddling their wares, but as he walked along he saw none. Stopping by a shoeshine stand where an old man was hawking customers, he sat down—not for a shine, especially, but for information.

"What's become of the apple sellers? Don't they work on weekends?"

"They got priced right out, suh. The suppliers kept rising their cost and cutting their profits, which wasn't much to start out. And the apples wasn't as good as before, neither. Time was I could hardly set myself up here for them lined up a-cloggin' up the whole sidewalk. . . . You here on bidness, suh?"

"No, just taking a look around on my way to Washington," Jack said. He paid the man a nickel and went on his way, consulting a list he'd made up. There were so many buildings he wanted to see that were new since he'd last been here. First on the list was the Empire State Building. It had been built the year before and was the tallest building in the world. He'd spotted it towering over the city landscape from a distance on the train and wanted to look at it close-up.

There was only a four-hour gap between his arrival and departure times, so he could see only a few: the Chrysler Building, built in 1930; the newly completed RCA Victor, the Ritz Tower, and half a dozen others were all on his list. It would be a challenge to decide which to see.

He couldn't figure out how, in the deepening financial depression, anyone could afford to put up new buildings. New York City really was a world unto itself. He passed a movie house that looked like a palace and was showing a new James Cagney film. Several people had mentioned that Jack faintly resembled the actor, and he never missed one of Cagney's talkies when they finally got to Voorburg. It broke his heart to pass this one by.

He was disappointed slightly by the Empire State Building. It was turning into a brutally hot, humid, cloudy day, and he couldn't see the top of it from the street. Maybe there was an elevator to the top and the clouds might clear. But in the spectacular lobby, he gave up. The building was still so new that mobs of people with children filled the waiting area, to visit and ride the free elevators. He'd waste too much time.

He stepped back outside, consulting his notes for addresses to find out which of his other chosen sites was closest.

"I'm going to have to go down to the city today with this suit," Chief Walker said to Robert. "You *are* coming along with me, aren't you? I don't know New York City well."

"I do," Robert said. "Why can't you just telephone the establishment that made it and describe the suit?"

"I don't speak the language of clothing,"

Walker said. "I want them to take a look at it. It's a long shot, but the guy in Albany thought it was a good enough idea to have a toadie drive it down here early this morning. Poor fella must have had to start out at about three in the morning. And he has to take it back as well. Frankly, I think it's useless. No tailor would remember one of probably thousands of suits."

Robert disagreed. "Fine clothing makers are as obsessed as dentists about keeping records. They can trace a person just from the measurements in their files. They know when he started putting on weight, and how much he gained—and probably whether it was gained before or after his divorce."

"If you say so," Walker said.

When they got to Grand Central Station, Walker was agog. He tried to disguise his yokel reaction, but couldn't. "What a terrific heap!"

Robert was kind enough not to gloat over how many times he'd been here, and merely glanced at the address of the clothier. "It's quite a long walk up Fifth Avenue and it's too hot to hoof it. Want to take a cab?"

"Can we afford it?"

"It's a cab or new shoes for both of us. Take your pick."

The cabbie got stuck in traffic, so they bailed out a couple of blocks from their destination. When they reached the address they sought, the windows of the establishment were without glass and boarded up.

"Rats!" Robert exclaimed.

"I can hear something going on inside. Let's crash the party."

After much pounding on a locked door, a construction worker laden with a big charred plank opened it and said, "Yeah?"

"What happened to the shop that was here?" Walker asked. "I'm the Chief of Police of a town upriver and need some information."

The worker waved them in. "Burnt out, isn't it?" he said, pointing out the obvious.

Robert and Howard just looked at each other. "Is there anyone around today from the company that used to be here?"

"Maybe. They're trying to get it going again. Waste of time, but who am I to complain about having a job? There's a lanky blond guy hangs out most times, snooping to see if we're really working. Wears a brown suit. Help yourself and look around."

There must have been twenty men working, going in and out the back door, presumably to an alley, carrying away trash or bringing in carpentry tools and wood and cans of paint. They finally spotted the one man in a suit.

Howard cornered him delivering a tirade to a kid who'd dropped a paintbrush. "Be sure to clean that up before you use it. I'll be watching that you do."

After the boy had escaped, Howard Walker showed his badge, and introduced himself. "Do you work for the company that occupied these premises?"

"Of course I do. Would I be here in this rubble otherwise?" the man said, not even giving them his name.

Howard pretended with some effort that he was unaware of the man's rudeness. "Let me explain, if I may. We have an unidentified body and he's wearing one of your suits. We need someone in the company to measure it carefully and see if you have his name in your records. And maybe an address."

The man laughed. It was an ugly, vaguely victorious laugh. "All the records went up in flames. They were kept here, you see. Old Man Blackstone kept an eagle eye on everything. He even kept the records of men who'd died a generation ago, God knows why."

"Where does he live?"

"Just around the corner." He gave the address. "But it's useless. He's as dotty and mean as a drunk goat. Good luck, boys."

They found the four-story town house easily, but getting in was harder. A granite-eyed butler with a fake British accent guarded the portal. "Mr. Blackstone sees no one without an appointment. Do you have one?"

"No, but I'm the Law," Howard Walker said, just as pretentiously, "and I have the suit of a murdered man I need to show him." He thrust the paper bag into the arms of the butler. A sleeve dangled out, musty and dirty.

The butler held it at arm's length. "Mr. Blackstone won't be interested in this."

"Then I'll have to get a warrant and send the boys in blue to the door to deliver it. That won't look good to the neighbors."

The butler waffled, trying to force the bag back on Walker.

"Let the man himself decide if he will see us," Walker said. "We'll wait out here on the stoop."

"We call it a porch," the butler said, taking yet more umbrage.

"I live in a mansion that has a porch that puts yours to shame," Robert said loftily, "and I'm not the Law. I'm a third-generation customer."

That did it. The butler slammed the door but kept the bag.

"Are you really a third-generation customer of this outfit?" Walker asked.

Robert shrugged. "Never even heard of the place. I just hoped it would work."

It did.

The butler looked even angrier as he returned fifteen minutes later without the paper bag. As if he'd forgotten the previous encounter, he said stiffly, "Mr. Blackstone will see you in the library."

The elderly Mr. Blackstone, wearing an ancient black velvet smoking jacket, white hair askew, had cleared off a big table, laid out the suit, and was examining it with a magnifying glass and a long ruler. If he was as dotty as his underling implied, he must have been having an especially lucid day.

He glanced up briefly, assessing their garb. Walker wasn't in uniform, but Mr. Blackstone knew suits. He immediately dismissed Walker on the basis of his clothing.

"That's an old one you've got on, son," he said to Robert. "Who are you?"

"I'm a Brewster and my mother was a Vanderbilt," Robert half lied.

The old man nodded. "But you didn't stay with us, did you? We never would have made a suit that fit that badly."

"I've lost weight since it was made," Robert said, unruffled by the tough old bird. Lots of his grandfather's old pals had gone a bit gaga in the social graces when they managed to pass their seventy-fifth birthday, and he wasn't intimidated by bad manners in the successful elderly crowd. He'd always been pretty good at jollying them along.

"This *is* our suit," Mr. Blackstone said, pointing at the one from the corpse. "So often people buy one, and their wives have their maids sew the label into a cheaper one when the man outgrows ours. The maids never do it right. Men tend to get heavier—and stingier—as they enter middle age. But I can tell by the way it's stitched that we put the label in."

"Could you make a guess at who it belonged to?" said Howard Walker, who never paid attention to whether suits had labels or not.

"I don't think so. But it wasn't a New Yorker. We put black labels in the suits of our regularly returning local customers. This is a dark gray. That means it was a first-time buyer from elsewhere. That was before we went to all-black labels because the yokels had figured out they weren't impressing the locals."

"When was the change made in the color of the labels?" Walker asked.

"May of 1923."

"So the person was alive then?"

Mr. Blackstone cackled horribly. "We seldom have the necessary time between death and burial to make our customers a new suit. We provide quality, not speed. Though we've done so on rare occasions. The last time was for one of 'your' Vanderbilts," he intoned gruffly, looking at Robert, making clear that he didn't believe his genealogical remarks.

"Could you tell us this person's size?" Howard Walker asked, tired of the snobby contest being conducted by the other two men.

"He must have been approximately five foot eleven and a quarter. Weighing—I'd guess— about two hundred seven pounds. Long-legged and short-waisted with heavy shoulders and the beginning of a paunch."

"Approximately five foot eleven and a quarter," Robert said with a chuckle.

"That could be a lot of men," Walker said.

"The suit very well might not have been made

for the person you found wearing it," Mr. Black-stone said. "These days lots of clothing gets passed down to the more unfortunate."

The two men thanked Mr. Blackstone effu-sively for his opinions, snubbed the butler, and were soon back on the street with the suit in its paper bag.

"What a waste of time!" Walker said.

"Not necessarily. We have an approximate date of purchase—at least a last date of purchase—and a rough idea of his physique in life. It's more than we knew this morning."

"Unless Mr. Blackstone was right about the suit being a hand-me-down," Walker said, with a frown.

Chapter 8

Jack Summer arrived in Washington, D.C., on Saturday night just after eight. The weather was stifling. He caught his breath and wondered why the center of the U.S. government had been built on a swamp. What were the Founding Fathers thinking? Anywhere else would have been better. What had been wrong with Philadelphia? Even a few miles away from here there were hills where at least you might catch the occasional breeze that didn't stink of rotting fish and sewage.

It was the height of summer, and the air was heavy, fetid, and foul. Dragging along his battered old suitcase of clothing and his notebook, he started out from the train station and had to stop periodically just to wipe his brow with an already damp, grubby handkerchief. He checked his map at every street he passed. At least he knew where he was going, the office of Superintendent of Police Pelham Glassford.

The office would probably be closed this late on a Saturday, but someone would be around to direct him to the men he wanted to find. He hoped that on Monday he could interview Glassford. He was a good man. He'd been in the thick of battle himself in the Great War, had welcomed the Bonus Army to Washington, and housed the first contingent in some abandoned office buildings in the city. He'd raised funds, including a generous amount of his own salary, to set the men up in what comfort he could.

There were men in groups all over the streets, so Jack asked one who'd just given directions to someone else, "How can I find people I'm looking for here?"

The man, who wasn't much older than Jack himself, wore no uniform or badge and wasn't nearly old enough to have served in the Great War, but he exuded authority. "It depends on when your friends came here. There are more than twenty encampment areas. They're sorted by state or region of the state."

"About three weeks ago, I think."

"Then they're not in the city proper. Only the first to arrive are close. They'll be over on the Anacostia Flats. That's the largest compound and the most recent arrivals are there, about fifteen thousand of them."

Jack gasped. "Fifteen thousand! How will I ever find the right people?"

"It's well laid out, and they have rough maps.

The entrance encampment on the other side of the Eleventh Street Bridge can help you. They're mostly all U.S. Army, including lots of former officers, you realize. They know how to organize huge numbers of people, and army folks love maps."

"How do I get there?" Jack asked.

"Do you know where Pennsylvania Avenue is?"

"Yes."

"Take it southeast, about a mile and a half, and turn right on Eleventh Street. It'll take you right to the bridge. About a two-mile walk is all."

In the spring or fall at home in Voorburg this wouldn't have seemed like any distance at all. But in a sweltering, smelly July night in Washington, when he'd been up since before dawn and had already walked all over midtown Manhattan, it seemed a very long way.

Jack thanked the young man and started out, feet literally dragging, and the suitcase feeling twice as heavy as it did this morning.

He found his way easily and was surprised at how much traffic there was going the same way. Men were still arriving in cars and trucks, on foot, and even by bicycle, with most of them, like him, on foot. Some had farm wagons pulled by horses or mules. Many had their wives and children in tow. It had never occurred to Jack that women and children were involved in this, and he'd not read or heard another commentator mention them. But why not? They had every bit as much at stake in demonstrating to the government how desperately they needed the bonus payment to survive—*now!* Not thirteen years from now.

But there were also a few people going the other way, men and women who couldn't face looking at the newcomers. They had grim expressions and looked away from the people joining the marchers. They were those who'd given up and were going home, Jack assumed. Jack hadn't even reached his destination, and to his utter shame he was vaguely considering turning around and going back to Voorburg.

The main encampment tent across the Eleventh Street Bridge crossing the Anacostia River was well staffed. The first line he stood in was managed by an older man with a spectacular reddish mustache that flared out when he spoke. "Where are these folks you're looking for from?" he asked Jack.

"New York. Voorburg-on-Hudson."

The gentleman, still able to fit into his Great War uniform and wearing it with pride, even though he hadn't been able to get rid of the creases from its having been folded away for well over a decade, flipped through a couple of registers. "I don't see a listing for this town. Is it small? What's it near?"

"I guess it is pretty small," Jack had to admit, against his will. "It's between Cold Spring and Poughkeepsie."

"Ah, that makes it easier." He pulled out a

stack of crudely hand-drawn maps and handed one to Jack. "This is the general layout. And here," he said, circling a distant area, "is where you need to go. There'll be a sign with this number on a tall stake, and someone will be stationed there who knows where your friends are."

Jack was sick at heart at how far away it looked. He had been hoping as he crossed the bridge that the end of his journey was close. But he was also pleased and encouraged by how well this movement was functioning. No one was apparently being paid to do the work, but here were lots of middle-aged men—some in heavy wool uniforms from their war years, some in farm clothes and muddy boots, and a few in shabby dress suits—volunteering to help newcomers. He himself was so tired and hot that the thought nearly brought him to tears, a feeling he hadn't experienced in many years.

A young woman with a long blond braid carrying a baby in a sling made with a pretty shawl and holding the hand of an older child overtook him. It embarrassed him that, thus burdened, she walked faster than he did. "You look lost," she said, pausing. "May I help you?"

"Yes, please," he said cravenly, handing over his map with his destination marked.

"You're going the right way. Follow me. You're Jack Summer, aren't you?"

He stared at her. "How did you know my name?"

"We live in Voorburg, with my grandfather. I couldn't let him come to this horrible place alone. He's not in good health, and I knew he wouldn't take his medicine if I wasn't here to nag him. I'm Mary Towerton. My grandad's Joseph Wyman."

"Oh, he's a swell old man," Jack said. "Is your husband with you as well?"

"No. He went off to work on that big Boulder Dam in Arizona or Nevada, one of those western places, months ago. We haven't heard from him since." There was a frisson of panic in her voice. "Come along. Grandad will be happy to see you."

Jack was lying tactfully by calling Old Joe Wyman a swell old man. Old Joe was a lush and a bully, and this nice young woman must know it better than anyone. He was legendary for his violent rages and mule-headed ignorance.

"Who's in charge of the Voorburg contingent?" he asked breathlessly.

She slowed her pace for his sake. "Johnson Spelling. Corporal Spelling, he was once. Do you know him?"

"Only by name. He lives outside town, doesn't he? A bit north."

She hitched up the baby, who was starting to mewl like a frightened kitten, and said, "That's right. I'll show you to his tent, and he'll assign you to stay with someone. Probably us. Everybody else has given up on staying with Grandad."

And so it proved to be, unfortunately.

"I'm sorry, Summer," ex–Corporal Spelling

said, with genuine regret, "but everyone else is too crowded already. I know the old buzzard is a real son of a bitch, but all our people have tried to get along with him and now it's your turn as the latecomer. If anyone leaves, I'll try to get you in their spot. I hear there's a bunch from Beacon who are talking about going home because their crops need harvesting. Here's a map of our section— latrines, mess hall, drill area, and the medical hut in the encampment next door. Keep it handy. And stay well away from Old Joe. He's got a big oak cane and thoroughly thrashed the last guy I put in with his family."

"Thanks," Jack said weakly.

Saturday evening, when Phoebe came home to Grace and Favor, she hunted down Lily. "I have a message for you. Mrs. White has called another special meeting for tomorrow afternoon. I guess she heard from her cousin about the truck store rules."

"Oh, dear. I was hoping it would take longer."

"I think everyone hoped so," Phoebe said. "I could tell her that you've already promised to help Mrs. Prinney with her garden. I'll take notes."

Lily slapped her forehead. "Oh, dear. I haven't had my conversation yet about the garden."

Phoebe looked puzzled.

"It's nothing, really. Just something I heard that I've got to pass on to Mrs. Prinney, and she won't much like hearing it. But I'd appreciate it a lot if you could take along my excuse to Mrs. White."

"I will. There's really no point in both of us going, I suppose. I've got to shower and change for dinner."

Lily mentally girded her loins and went out to help Mrs. Prinney with the weeding. "May I help?" she asked.

"No, dear. You don't know a weed from a lettuce."

The heavyset older woman was so red in the face that Lily was alarmed. "Go sit down for a while and I'll fix a lemonade for you."

"We're out of lemons," Mrs. Prinney said, heaving herself up with difficulty from her crouching position on her little gardening rug and putting both hands to her back.

"Then some nice cool water, at least," Lily said.

When she returned, Mrs. Prinney was sitting in one of the Adirondack chairs in the shade, fanning herself ineffectually with an empty seed packet. Her color was a little better.

"I have something I'm going to hate telling you, but I promised to do so."

"Oh, dear . . ."

"When I was in town yesterday, Mr. Bradley spoke to me about you. He's frightened that you're setting a trend he fears others will follow." Lily invented a softer phrase he hadn't exactly used.

"What does that mean?" Mrs. Prinney said,

wiping her brow with a freshly laundered and ironed handkerchief she pulled from her capacious bosom. She kept a lot of things there: a small bottle of camphor oil, a tiny tin of aspirin, and heaven knew what else.

"He says if you grow your own vegetables you'll cut down on his business. He fears he'll lose other customers as well, who learn to do as you do."

Mrs. Prinney stared at Lily. "That's absurd. There are still things I simply can't grow. It takes a good three or four years to get a decent asparagus bed to produce, I'm told. Longer for a lemon tree to produce fruit, even if we keep it in the conservatory in the winter."

"But, Mrs. Prinney, I can see his point, I'm afraid. His stock-in-trade is mainly the same things you're growing—beans, peas, carrots, tomatoes, and lettuce. He counts on our business to keep his shop going. He believes that we're all rich and stingy and thoughtless, I'm sorry to say. You'd feel awful if you were responsible, even in part, to putting him on the dole."

Mrs. Prinney said nothing for a long moment. She merely stared at her garden. Then she heaved a sigh. "I suppose you're right. My vegetables aren't turning out as well as I'd hoped, anyway. It's too hard to keep up with the watering, let alone the weeding. The carrots I've pulled are already a bit gnarly. Not nearly as good as those Mrs. Anderson grows and sells to him. And they won't be ready to eat until October, if ever. And I can't keep the lettuces from wilting every afternoon. And the bugs and deer eat the best things every night. I have to admit I'm sorry I started this. It's too much work for me."

"I'm glad you feel that way. I've worried about what it's doing to your health, too."

"I hate to let it go, but between the pests and the time it takes and the poor results so far, I suppose I should abandon it. I'll run to town tomorrow morning and tell Mr. Bradley I'm giving it up."

Lily rose from where she was sitting on the grass. "You're doing a very noble thing, Mrs. Prinney."

"Just a moment, dear. Give me a hand getting out of this chair. I think I'm stuck to it."

Chapter 9

By the time they got to church in the morning, Mrs. Prinney was in full flight, telling everyone she was giving up her garden in support of Mr. Bradley. The citizens of the town were obligated to help their own people keep in business. She didn't actually say it was immoral to grow your own food but came as close as she could to expressing this view. She was very noble about it.

But she was also careful not to offend Roxanne Anderson. Mrs. Prinney raved about Mrs. Anderson's garden and the fact that she was selling her very fine excess produce to Mr. Bradley and helping him out.

Lily suspected strongly that Mrs. Prinney had secretly been waiting for someone to give her a good reason to stop torturing herself with a vegetable garden, and Lily had provided it.

But it left Lily with no valid excuse to miss Mrs. White's emergency meeting. The residents of

Grace and Favor went home from church to the best Sunday dinner they'd had in a long while, since Mrs. Prinney was no longer giving all her attention to the garden and had gone back to what she did best—spectacular cooking. In the afternoon Robert would drive Lily and Phoebe down the hill to Mrs. White's and pick them back up.

"So long as I don't have to deliver you two to the door and talk to her," he specified.

"Why would she want to talk to you?" Lily said with a laugh.

"I hear she's very good at getting people to do what she wants. And I've heard nasty rumors about someone having to drive around in a truck. Not my cup of tea. Is that what the meeting's about?"

"I'm afraid so," Lily said. "What did you and Chief Walker learn about that suit yesterday? And why did it take you until midnight to get home?"

"We stopped off at one of my favorite speakeasies in the city. I practically had to pour Howard onto the train. But we didn't learn much about the suit. The old boy who ran the business had lost his records in a fire. He did give us a physical description of the person it was made for, though."

"That's some help isn't it?"

"Unfortunately not. The man wearing the suit might have been given it when the original owner outgrew it or simply got tired of wearing it. You gave some of your clothes to Mimi when we came here because you'd lost weight and the clothes were out of style by then. Remember?"

"True. So how else can the victim be identified? Will the pathology guy in Albany be able to tell how long ago he died? Or match up his teeth or something?"

"I have no idea," Robert said. "But I can't let it go. Everybody in town knows we found a body in the old icehouse. We've got to be able to explain it."

Lily didn't quite understand why this was Robert's responsibility, and certainly it was not hers, but if he felt so strongly, she'd go along without arguing.

The women straggled into the meeting, none of them happy with giving up part of their Sunday to this traveling truck idea. Once again, Roxanne was the last to show up. She seemed to be the busiest of all of them. Poor young Ruby Heggan had brought her baby and looked haggard. She was upset at being pregnant again, and Lily wondered if her husband was still seriously considering driving them clear to California. What a hideous trip that would be for Ruby. But at least she'd get away from her husband's awful brothers.

Nina Pratt looked pretty cranky as well. Sunday was her only day off from the beauty shop to do things with her daughter, and she mentioned twice that to attend this meeting she'd given up a trip to Poughkeepsie to visit an old uncle.

Even Susan Gasset, who'd been so funny and cheerful about her popcorn-smelling hair and their diet of rabbits, wasn't herself. "We aren't going to have to stay and do our sewing today, are we?" she asked Edith. "This is the day I do all my washing and ironing."

Henry White dropped in on the meeting again. "A Sunday meeting? I can hardly believe it. Isn't my wife a wonder?"

"Oh, Henry, how you *do* go on." Edith actually blushed, something Lily suspected nobody had ever seen happen before. "Now scoot. We've got things to discuss. It won't take long." She gave him a look that suggested they had very intimate plans for the afternoon.

The minute he left, chuckling to himself, Edith came right back to where the conversation at the last Ladies League meeting had left off, though first she daintily blotted a bit of a sheen off her upper lip. "No, Susan. We're not sewing today. I just want to give you a report from my cousin so we can get on with the traveling shop," Edith answered, apparently unaware that nobody was thrilled with her summons.

When everyone was present, Edith started reading from her notes about how the scrip exchange worked. Lily had given up trying to understand it because Edith was obviously going to see that it was done with or without anyone else's approval.

There was no point in trying to grasp the concept or try to improve it in the face of such determination. Glancing around the room as Edith cheerfully and tediously laid out a complex set of rules, Lily realized the rest of them appeared to have come to the same conclusion.

Phoebe seemed to be feverishly taking notes, but Lily suspected she was really sketching out hats she planned to make.

Poor Peggy Rismiller, the minister's wife, who'd put in a good three hours greeting churchgoers this morning, looked as if she might fall asleep at any moment. Lily had heard that since so many of the parishioners could no longer be as financially supportive of the church as they used to be, they'd worked out a round-robin program of inviting the minister and his wife to a big Sunday dinner each week of the year. The Rismillers must have found this rotating hospitality somewhat of a trial in addition to all their other community activities.

Lily herself felt sleepy but was kept from napping by a tiny sound behind her. She turned slightly to look out the window and saw Chief Howard Walker standing so that nobody else could see him. He gestured to her to come outside.

Lily said, "Will you ladies please excuse me for a moment," without explanation, and went out the front door where Walker was now standing.

"What are you doing peeking through windows?"

"I understand Mrs. Anderson's at this meeting."

"Yes?"

"Could you manage to have her come out here?"

"I suppose so. What's this about?"

He didn't reply.

Lily went back inside and leaned over Roxanne's shoulder and whispered, "Someone needs to see you outside."

"Has something happened to my children or my brother?"

"I don't know," Lily replied.

Without another word, Roxanne hurried out the front door, and a few moments later there was a horrifying scream.

Lily was the first to get outside. Roxanne was pounding on Chief Walker's chest and sobbing. "No, no, no! It can't be true!"

Walker looked at Lily with a "help me" glance as he gently tried to grab Roxanne's wrists. Lily snagged one of Roxanne's hands and tugged. Roxanne whirled around and fell into Lily's arms so violently they almost toppled to the ground. By this time the rest of the women had come outside and were standing in a confused, alarmed clump on the porch.

"What's this all about?" Edith White demanded.

Walker removed his hands from his aching temples and said, "Mrs. Anderson's husband has been found dead in the woods near the railroad tracks."

Roxanne, who had been clinging desperately to Lily, and keening like a fatally injured animal, sank to her knees.

Jack Summer spent Saturday night in the tent with Joe Wyman and his granddaughter and her children. Old Joe was so tired and sick with the heat that he didn't even notice. Mary made Jack a thin pallet on the floor in the corner out of a couple of their extra blankets and some clothing. It was unbearably hot, and he was as far from the open tent flap as it was possible to be.

He hardly got any sleep at all. Joe snored like a freight train, gasping and snorting horribly all night long. About two in the morning the baby started crying, and Mary accidentally stepped on Jack's hand in the dark. She took the child to the opposite corner of the tent, sat down on a stool with her back to everyone, and started nursing the baby. The sound made Jack unbearably uncomfortable when he was already miserable. He'd slept in all his dirty, sweaty clothing, feeling this was only decent in the presence of a woman, and could hardly bear his own smell.

He had finally dropped into a fitful nap about dawn when some idiot with a bugle played reveille—badly—just outside the tent, almost making Jack's heart stop. The camp came awake. There were sounds of people calling to each other and dishes and pans clanking in the mess hall across the way.

Jack gave up on sleeping and went in search of Corporal Snelling. "Where can I wash out my clothes and clean myself up?"

Snelling, who already looked as bright and tidy as a button, pointed the way but said, "You should go to the mess hall first before they run out of food."

"I'd rather be clean," Jack said, sounding surly even to himself.

When he'd washed and shaved as well as he could in a basin of tepid water, put on fresh clothes, rinsed out the clothing he'd worn the day before, and hung his shirt and trousers and underwear on a handy clothesline among many other people's laundry, he started feeling a little bit better. As the smell of the food drew him to the mess tent, he realized he was lucky to be housed in a tent. Most of the other "structures" were big cardboard boxes, packing crates, tar paper stretched over branches and sticks, and even a piano case, most of which had been foraged from the city dump.

The first person he spotted in the mess tent was Edwin McBride. Edwin had served in the Great War as a very young man and formerly was an accountant, but now he worked as a porter at the Voorburg train station. He was one of the gabbiest people in town.

"Why, if it isn't Jack Summer!" he called. "Come sit yourself down. What the hell are you doing here?"

"Looking for you and the other men and their families from Voorburg," Jack said, sitting down on the army-issued plank bench beside Edwin. "I want to interview each of you about why you're here."

Edwin bellowed across the room to three other local men and gestured to them to bring their plates over to talk to Jack. Not that they had much luck, because Edwin never stopped to let anyone else speak.

"I suppose you know who started this?" he said to Jack, and before Jack could reply, he went on. "Back in May a former medic in Portland, Oregon, organized about three hundred other vets thereabouts, and they stole a train engine and couple of boxcars and set out for Washington. The guy's name was Walter Waters and the group named him their leader and headed clear 'cross the country, picking up more vets and trains as they went. That Waters guy's a good speaker. We've taken to calling him General Waters. He'd stop at every little town along the way and fire the men up about what they'd taken to calling the Bonus Expeditionary Force, or BEF. Clever, eh? Like the AEF—the American Expeditionary Force in the war."

Edwin shoved a piece of toast in his mouth quickly and went on without a break, chewing while he spoke.

"Towns took up funds to rent boxcars and send their vets to Washington. Seven hundred or more vets made their way down from Philadelphia. A bunch of Tennessee folks also came in boxcars, along with a goat named Hoover."

Edwin chuckled, spewing a few crumbs.

"So here we all are, sitting it out. We're planning to stay here until 1945 if we have to. A week and a half ago was the best day of all so far. The House, bless 'em, voted to pass the Patman bill and pay us the bonus money. But the Senate overruled it. General Waters was called in to be told.

"Nearly half the BEF showed up to hear what he had to say when he came out of the Senate room. He said we'd had a little setback and we'd all hold out for better news, and someone in the crowd started singing 'America,' and everyone else joined in. I tell you, Summers, I damn near cried my eyes out. All those men and women taking it on the chin like that, singing 'America.' "

Edwin paused again briefly to take a big spoonful of coarse oatmeal, and one of the other men got a chance to speak.

"I don't call him General Waters. I call him a fascist. His head's gotten as big as a dirigible. He's got bodyguards and has set up his own military police force and is talking big about what great fellows Hitler and Mussolini are to rise through the ranks like he has and take control. He said so in the camp newsletter, and he couldn't even spell Hitler's name right. He's turned into a menace to the cause."

Edwin had been uttering liquid mews of dismay throughout this speech. "It don't matter if he can't spell right. Only someone like you, a teacher, cares about that kind of stuff."

A third man said, "I'd rather call Glassford 'General.' He's the Bonus Army Expedition's treasurer. It's him who's collecting the money to feed us, from towns and bigwigs and ordinary people all over the country who send a dollar bill or two to help us out."

Jack wasn't eating. He was furiously scribbling down everything that was being said.

Chapter 10

"I want to go home," Roxanne sobbed. "I have to tell the children and my brother."

Walker said, "Your brother knows. I went to your house first, and he told me you were here. Robert Brewster has his car. We'll take you home."

Until then, Lily hadn't noticed the Duesie sitting on the street with Robert at the wheel.

"She'll need a woman along," Mrs. White said from the porch, and started toward them.

"Yes," Walker said. "Lily, will you go with us?" He herded the two women into the Duesie before Mrs. White could interfere.

They got Roxanne in the backseat with Lily and sped off. "Does your brother live with you?" Lily asked.

Roxanne stared at her for a moment, red-eyed, as if having to concentrate on processing the question. "Yes, he's a widower. His wife died of tuberculosis last year, and he and his daughter came to live with us. He can't find work, but he helps take care of the children when I leave the house, and he does all the heavy work in the garden. Chief Walker, how did my husband die?"

"We'll talk about this when we get you home with your family," Walker said.

Lily had never been to the Andersons' house. It was about halfway up the hill on a road she'd never been on. It was big but shabby. It badly needed painting, a screen door was askew, and there was a broken window on the second floor. The land ran uphill slightly behind the house and then quickly became very steep, but there was a large flat area in front, filled entirely with the vegetable garden. A tall wall of roughly hewn stones kept the garden from eroding into the drive.

"Stop for a moment," Roxanne said, at the bottom of the gravel drive. "I can't let the children see me like this."

Lily had a fresh handkerchief in the pocket of her dress and gave it to Roxanne, who mopped her eyes and face, blew her nose, sat up straight, and composed herself with an obvious effort.

"I'm ready now," she said.

Robert pulled up the drive to the front door, where a tall man was standing. Roxanne got out of the car, the rest following a decent distance behind her. The man came down the steps and embraced her silently.

Roxanne turned and said, "This is my brother,

Eugene." She introduced the others to him. "Do the children know?" she asked her brother.

He shook his head no.

"Could you take them outside to play in back? I'll tell them later," Roxanne said.

Eugene went and gathered them up, while the rest of them waited outside. Then they entered the house.

"I'll fix some coffee," Lily said. "I think we all need some."

Roxanne collapsed in a chair in the front room with a colorful hand-knitted throw over it while Lily went to the kitchen. Eugene had already started the coffee and Lily hunted down cups for the four of them, putting them on a tray. The kitchen was spotless, the old dishes neatly stacked. Roxanne was a good housekeeper as well as a good gardener.

Through the kitchen window she could see Eugene playing a game with the children on the hill behind the house. She'd never seen or met him before and wondered if he was a bit simple. He was big, older than Roxanne, apparently, slow to move, and hadn't spoken. He kept warily looking back at the house.

Lily put spoons, cups, sugar, and the last of a bottle of milk on a tray and went back to the front room.

Roxanne took an obligatory sip and said to Walker, "Tell me."

"What's your husband's first name, Mrs. Anderson?"

"Donald."

Walker wrote it down in his notebook, as if he hadn't known it already. "And his age?"

"Thirty-seven."

Walker wrote this down as well and said, "I'm so sorry this has happened. He sustained a sharp blow to his temple."

There was a long silence before Roxanne asked, "How?"

"We don't know yet. It appears that it might have been administered by someone else. There's no sign that he fell on anything where he was found, and I have my men looking through the woods for a weapon."

Roxanne put her hands over her face for a long moment, then looked up. "Are you telling me he was murdered?"

"It's too soon to say for sure, but that's my first impression," Walker said softly. "I could be wrong."

"Who would do such a thing?"

"That's what we'll find out, if the coroner agrees it wasn't an accident. Mrs. Anderson, I hate making this harder for you, but you need to answer some questions."

She mopped her face again and sighed deeply.

"When was the last time you saw Donald?"

"Yesterday morning. He went off as usual to look for work."

"And he didn't come home last night?"

"Sometimes he didn't," she said. "If he'd gone a long way to find a job, he'd stay over—camping out in the woods or staying with a family he was working for, so he could start over in the morning if he hadn't found other work to do. No point in walking clear home, just to start out again in the morning."

"But today is Sunday. Where would he find work on a Sunday?"

"People often want work done on their house or yard on Sundays when they're home and can supervise. He wasn't used to manual labor, but he'd take any job he could find."

"What did he do when he was employed before?"

"He was a salesman for a hardware company. He traveled all over the state, selling farm implements to farmers and retailers."

Lily wondered if this was relevant or whether Walker was asking just to calm her down and get her talking.

"Did he have enemies?"

So much for the theory of calming her down, Lily thought.

Roxanne looked shocked at the question. "Of course not. When he still had his job, he was very friendly and amiable. That's what made him a good salesman. Everybody liked him."

"And when he lost his job?"

"He was unhappy. Who wouldn't be?" Roxanne said defensively. "A man without a job with a family to support is bound to become cranky. But he only showed it at home. He still had to pretend to be friendly when looking for work. At least I suppose so."

"Did he go out every day?"

"Yes. He dressed up in a suit and carried work clothes along in a big flat satchel. Sometimes he'd stay home on Sundays. But every other day he was gone, from early in the morning until darkness fell."

"Did he bring money home?" Walker prodded.

"Not often. You know as well as I do how hard it is to find work these days. Nobody can afford to pay casual labor. But he kept trying. It was better for him than sitting around the house feeling useless."

Walker stood and so did Robert. "I won't bother you anymore just now. I know how hard this is for you, and you need to be with your family. But I may have more questions, and I'll come back to let you know what we're finding out. Do you have a telephone?"

"We do, but it doesn't work anymore. We couldn't afford to pay for it."

Lily spoke up. "Do you want me to stay, Roxanne?"

"That's nice of you to offer, but no. I need to talk to the children. And I don't know how to tell them. I need time alone to think this out."

"Send your brother to fetch me if you need company, then," Lily said. "I'll be happy to come any time you want me or to bring a good friend if you'd like."

"I haven't had time to have friends for the last three years," Roxanne said. "Except for the ladies in the VLL."

Walker, Lily, and Robert headed back to town. "Poor Roxanne!" Lily said.

"She might be better off without him," Walker said.

"What an awful thing to say! He was her husband! Now she's a widow," Lily exclaimed.

"You didn't know him," Walker replied. "He wasn't quite as good a man as she portrayed him."

"Criminal?" Robert asked.

"No official record, if that's what you mean," Walker said. "But a heavy drinker on occasion and a bit of bully when he was drunk."

"So in spite of what Roxanne said, and maybe believes, he may well have had enemies?" Lily asked.

"It wouldn't surprise me a bit," Walker said. "Thanks for coming along. I'm not good with hysterical women."

"Is this all you know about him?" Lily persisted.

"It's all I'm willing to say," Walker said curtly. "I'm not allowed to gossip."

But I am, Lily thought.

"Lily, I'll take you back to Grace and Favor and drop you off," Robert said.

"No, leave me in town. I'll walk up the hill. I've got some errands to do." Before anyone could ask her about these theoretical errands, she added, "What have you learned about Robert's mummy?"

"Not much," Robert said. "We sent along what the tailor said about the size and proportions of the man who owned the suit. The coroner says the height is about right, but he can't tell about the shape. The muscles and organs shrink when a body dries out that way."

Once again, Lily was sorry she'd asked.

Chapter 11

Lily went back to Mrs. White's house, thinking some of the women might still be there and should know what happened. But no one was home at the White household except the maid, who said, "Mr. White's driven Mrs. White up to the Andersons' with a potato salad and a roast ready to go in the oven. And some milk and cookies for the children. She should be home soon, Miss Brewster, if you want to wait."

"No, thanks. I may come back later and see if I can catch her."

She really didn't intend to do this. Edith White would get the whole story out of Roxanne.

Nobody would be in town to gossip with on a late Sunday afternoon. Voorburg was a virtual ghost town then. The thought made Lily shiver. If the economy got worse, the Brewsters and the Prinneys might be the only ones left. She shook this thought away, saving it to brood over later.

For now she was convinced that if Donald Anderson had in fact been murdered, it would be sheer gossip that solved the case. On Monday she'd catch up with some of the women as they did their shopping. She realized that in cases of murder most often the spouse was the first suspect, and she hoped to find out something about Donald Anderson that would spare Roxanne Anderson that additional horror. She had come to like Roxanne a great deal in their short acquaintance. She was a woman who took charge of her life. Lily aspired to be the same kind of woman— so long as she didn't turn into an Edith White. The thought made her smile.

Since the day had grown hotter and hotter, the prospect of walking clear up the hill was daunting. She'd go down by the railroad tracks and see if Robert and the Duesie were still in town.

"Where's the satchel?" Walker asked, as he got out of Robert's car and approached his two deputies. As he sometimes did, he'd hired Harry Harbinger to be a temporary deputy. Harry was the elder of the two boys who'd been helping Robert take down the icehouse. He'd been a senior with the best grades in the county and headed for college in the fall of 1930, but he'd had to give this up to help the family. He was a very bright young man. Harry often helped with routine paperwork when Ralph Summer was off duty, because Ralph, the only full-time deputy, could hardly spell his own name, and his forms ended up looking as if they'd been wrapped around a sandwich.

Robert quietly followed Walker, not wanting to appear to be interfering but wanting to know what the deputies had been up to.

"What satchel?" Ralph asked.

"Mrs. Anderson said Donald always took along a satchel with his work clothes to save wear and tear on the suit he wore when he was looking for a job," Walker explained, wanting to smack Ralph. It was a characteristic of Donald Anderson that nearly everyone had noticed.

"You're right. I've seen him often with that satchel," Harry Harbinger said. "I didn't see it anywhere today, but I wasn't looking for it."

"What have you found while I was taking Mrs. Anderson home?" Walker asked. He knew he should really have stayed on the site where the body was found, but he hadn't wanted one of these young men to be the one to break the news to the victim's wife. Ralph would have botched it, and it would have broken Harry's heart.

"He was moved," Harry Harbinger said. Ralph was too busy chewing his gum to speak up. "There's a trail of blood coming from farther north along the tracks."

"Past that slight curve?" Walker asked, nodding.

"Yes, where you can't see from town what's behind the woods," Harry said.

"I wonder why he wasn't just left there?" Walker mused.

"Because the woods ain't as thick there," Ralph Summer explained, having put his gum behind his ear for future use.

"I'll take a look," Walker said. "You two come along and hunt along the edge of the woods for the satchel while we're at it. Don't step on the evidence of him having been moved. Robert, you come with me."

The trail was easy to follow. There weren't footprints as such, just scuffs in the dirt and crushed weeds. Robert and Howard Walker walked a safe distance from each side of the obvious path that led from where Donald Anderson had been left to the site of the attack.

"Who found him?" Robert asked.

"Two old guys in a railroad handcar checking sleepers due for replacement."

"Sleepers?" Robert asked. "Oh, you mean railroad ties," he added, saving himself from appearing an utter idiot. "Too bad there hasn't been any rain recently."

Walker nodded. "Apparently the person who moved the body couldn't carry it and had to drag it along. The body itself would have wiped out any footprints anyway."

But there were streaks of blood that a suspicious eye could catch on some lighter-colored leaves and grass along the way. Walker had some small paper bags along and picked up a few of the leaves with a pair of tweezers.

"This probably won't provide much help. Most

likely, if they were typed, they'd match the victim, unless the perpetrator was injured as well," he told Robert. "But it's standard procedure."

The trail suddenly disappeared around the slight bulge of woods close to the track just as a freight train hauling coal thundered past. This must be where the attack had taken place, Walker thought. It was confirmed by a relatively clear area of ground where a large pool of blood had soaked into the soil and turned brown. He set the two young men who'd followed them, searching for signs of the satchel, to look more carefully in the lightly wooded area farther back from the tracks.

"If you find it, don't touch it," he called out. "There might be fingerprints from the attacker's tossing it away."

Walker stood near the site of the bloodstain and studied the surroundings carefully. It was a good place to commit a murder. The railroad track went straight north and south, but the woods immediately to the south, closer to town, were unusually dense, close to the tracks, and shielded any view of the relatively open area behind.

"Whoever did this had to know the railroad schedule," Robert said.

That hadn't yet occurred to Walker. "Right. If this was done in daylight, you wouldn't want a slow train coming in or out of Voorburg, either freight or passenger, to see what was going on."

"There aren't many early passenger trains

along here on Sunday mornings, I wouldn't think," Robert speculated.

Walker nodded again. "The attack could have taken place anytime overnight. I wonder if we can count on Doc Polhemus to be able to determine time of death accurately?"

Robert would have liked to tell Walker his impression of the skills of their local doctor and county coroner, but he let it go. Young Dr. Polhemus might be a good doctor, but he was a blabbermouth about his patients' ailments, which to Robert's mind outweighed his medical skills. "How would anyone be able to spot the victim here at night, though?" he said instead.

"If he—or she—was following him, it could be done by sound alone. Everything's so dry the weeds would rustle."

"He *or she*? You surely don't suspect Mrs. Anderson?" Robert said, horrified at the thought.

"Of course I do. She's a big strong woman. She damned near knocked the wind out of me, beating on my chest, after I told her."

"But . . ." Robert had to marshal his thoughts. "She went completely to pieces when she heard."

"That could have been rehearsed," Walker said. "And she recovered her composure pretty quickly. She's strong that way, too."

"You don't honestly consider her your prime suspect, do you?"

Walker looked at Robert long and hard. "I don't have a prime suspect. But a lot of murders have to do with family problems, so she can't be discounted."

"But she seems such a nice woman. Concerned for her brother and her children, working so diligently to keep them all afloat in hard times."

"I agree, Robert. But I can't eliminate anyone as a suspect just because I like or admire them. And I have virtually no information about what happened here yet. I'm certainly not going to peel her children off her apron and throw her in the jug until and unless I find evidence that she's the guilty party. It could be anyone at this point."

"I had no idea you were so cynical," Robert said.

"That's what I'm paid to be," Walker said. "To my sorrow."

Robert found Lily sitting in the Duesie, fanning herself irritably with a folded map of the State of New York, when he returned. "You gave up on walking home?"

She just looked daggers at him.

Robert didn't say anything until they were almost back to Grace and Favor. Then he slowed the car and said, "Howard Walker suspects Mrs. Anderson."

He expected Lily to be as outraged as he'd been.

"Of course he does," Lily said.

Robert slammed on the brakes. The Duesie shuddered to a halt and died. "You can't think that too?"

"I don't think she *did* it. But I can see why Walker has to consider her. Robert, you're not usually so naive."

"I'm not naive. I just find it creepy crackers that a hardworking woman should be in the limelight as a suspect in her own husband's murder."

"Has Howard determined that it was murder?" Lily asked.

"What else could it be?"

Lily thought for a moment. "He could have been walking alongside the tracks trying to hitch a ride on a freight and hit his head. Or something might have come off a train. You see enormous chunks of coal along the tracks. It could have really been an accident, you know."

"And then someone 'accidentally' dragged him off to where he was better concealed?"

"Oh," Lily said. "I didn't know that part. Why didn't you tell me before I made a fool of myself?"

Robert smiled as he got the Duesie running. "Because I like when that happens."

Chapter 12

Monday morning, Lily accompanied Phoebe
when she went to work in town. Most days Mr.
Prinney gave Phoebe a lift in his rackety black
Ford when he went to his town office, but today
he was working at home, so they took the path
down through the woods again.

"What do you know about Donald Anderson?"
Lily asked Phoebe.

Phoebe thought for a long time before saying,
"I'm not one to gossip, but I didn't like him
much. I don't know anyone, except Roxanne,
who did. People say he was once a nice man, a
good father and husband. But losing his job
changed him. Not that I knew him well. I kept
away from him after he came in the shop last
spring pretending he wanted to surprise his
wife with a nice new Easter hat and then made
remarks to me that were—inappropriate."

"What sort of remarks?"

"I'd rather not repeat them," Phoebe said, blushing to the roots of her bright red hair.

Lily was surprised at Phoebe's reaction but didn't question her further.

She stopped by Jack's office, as she'd promised him, checking for water leaks and mail so important that it had to be tended to immediately. When she left she spotted Ruby Heggan across the street and caught up to her.

"What are you doing in town?"

"Just borrowing a spool of thread from a friend of my mother-in-law's. I had to get out of that noisy house. Why do you ask?"

"I wondered if you were in a hurry. I'd like to ask you something."

"I'd love to sit down and rest for a minute," Ruby said. "Isn't it awful about Mr. Anderson? I feel so sorry for Roxanne."

"Let me carry the baby for a bit. We can walk down to the park. Mr. Anderson's death is what I'm wondering about. Did you know him? What did you think of him?"

Ruby was stretching her arms with the relief. She dropped them to her sides when Lily spoke. Her reaction was as slow and careful as Phoebe's. Finally Ruby said, "Do you remember the fete at Grace and Favor last spring?"

"Of course."

"I brought Baby over to where you and Mrs. Prinney were spreading out blankets so the little ones could nap. And I stayed there."

"I do recall," Lily said, wondering where this was leading.

"That's because of Mr. Anderson. He kept following me around, asking to hold Baby. And each time it was an excuse to touch me. Here," she added, gesturing to her chest. "He frightened me."

"Of course he did," Lily said, outraged that any man would try that with such a vulnerable young woman.

"I couldn't find where my husband had gone, so I stayed with you and Mrs. Prinney until he turned up. I knew Mr. Anderson wouldn't bother me that way in front of the two of you."

"Did you tell your husband about it?"

Ruby laughed. "*Heavens*, no! Louis would have blabbed to his brothers and they'd have killed the man."

Suddenly she heard what she'd said. "I didn't mean that, really."

"But you can see why someone did," Lily commented.

"He was an awful person," Ruby said, sitting down on the only remaining bench in the tiny park. She took a handkerchief out of her pocket and patted her forehead. "I shouldn't have told you. I've never told anyone else."

"I'm sorry I upset you. I didn't mean to," Lily said.

"No. I needed to say it sometime. I had nightmares about him for weeks after."

"Do you think Roxanne knew he behaved that way?"

Ruby shrugged. "I don't know. I hope she didn't. It would have really hurt her feelings. At least it would have hurt mine if I learned something like that about *my* husband."

So at least two of Lily's women acquaintances had been approached "inappropriately," as Phoebe had put it. Women who knew and liked his wife. If it had happened to Lily herself, she hoped she wouldn't have kept silent. She'd have at least threatened to tell Roxanne. Maybe. Or maybe she'd have been as humiliated as they'd been and kept silent.

As Lily jiggled Baby—surely that wasn't his actual name, Lily thought—and made him giggle, she said, "Let's go get a soft drink at Mabel's before you borrow your thread. My treat. It's so darned hot today."

On Monday morning Jack walked back to the city, hoping to get an interview with Superintendent Glassford. There was so much activity at the building where the man's office was that he hadn't a hope. He asked three people who looked authoritative if he could see the superintendent for just five minutes. The last of the three said, "See those guys at the end of the hall, about twenty of them? They're all reporters like you. And he hasn't time today to see anyone."

Jack trudged back to the camp across the river. He hadn't really expected much, but he was discouraged nonetheless—discouraged and hot,

sticky, and tired to death as well. The stench of latrines and garbage, the hordes of flies and mosquitoes, the dreadful food, the diseases that were
breaking out around him were about to make him
run back home to Voorburg.

But before he could leave, he had to justify having done this. He came here to interview the local
men, or at least some of them. He had to hunt
through what seemed to be half of humanity to
find the locals, but he finally managed to run
down the one who had been a teacher and asked
if he had time to talk.

"As if I had a job to go to," the man said bitterly. "What do you want to talk about? This?" he
gestured at the Hooverville of handmade tar-
paper shacks, boxes, crates, and tents made out of
old newspapers and strips of canvas stuck together with paste. "Is this any way for people to
live? Some men have been here since March or
April. And many have nothing better to go home
to. They have no homes anymore."

Jack felt someone owed this man an apology,
but it wasn't his job or his fault.

"You know the history of this movement, I assume," the man said. "By the way, my name's
George Newman. I didn't catch yours."

Jack introduced himself and they shook hands.

George led the way to the mess tent, empty
now of all but the staff, who were cleaning up,
and what seemed like millions of flies and an
equal number of mosquitoes.

George sat down, swatting randomly, and said, "Edwin McBride, the guy who was shooting off his mouth when you arrived, is a good man, but he's let the wool be pulled over his eyes. He's only recently out of work, and it hasn't gotten through to him that he's not going to get a job when he returns home any more than the rest of us will. He's gone from being a professional man to a porter working for tips that most people can't afford to give him. I'll grant, it was a touching moment when everyone sang 'America' together. But it didn't make any difference to Hoover and his toadies in the Senate. And it never will.

"You know, don't you, that Hoover's given orders, now that we've been offered the cost of part of our fare to go home, that we're going to be run out of Washington?"

"Do you really think so?"

"I know it. And the hundred thousand dollars he granted to get people home. Do you know where our esteemed President got that money?"

Jack couldn't bring himself to admit he didn't even know about the hundred-thousand-dollar bribe.

"He took it out of the bonus-money fund. Which has already been raided by this administration before. It'll come out of the amount that every single vet eventually gets in 1945—if there's anything left—whether the vet was here or not."

Jack was almost too stunned by this to write it down. He knew he wouldn't forget it, though.

"What else can he do?" George went on. "All this stupid talk of staying until 1945 is nonsense. You must have seen how many are already leaving as you got here. They were afraid of what would happen to them if they stayed."

"And you're not?" Jack asked.

"What the hell," George said. "My wife's given me up as a loss already. She's moved to Vermont and taken the children to her mother's. I can't get a job. My house is gone. I even had to sell my books to buy food to eat on the way here. What have I got to lose? I only wish . . ."

"Wish what?"

". . . that some of the rest of us who served together could have been here. We lost three good men in Voorburg after the Great War who might have knocked some sense into someone."

"Who were they? What happened to them?"

George quit scowling and swatting flies and said, "One of them—my best friend, in fact— was Butch O'Dwyer. He was really big and tough. One of the smartest men I ever knew, almost had his law degree when he joined up for the army. But he lost his right arm at Verdun and came home and drank himself to death. Just keeled over one night at Mabel's and was dead before he hit the floor. It was the second anniversary of the armistice. I think he willed himself to die that day."

Jack bowed his head, partly in tribute, mainly to jot down the name in his notes.

"Then there was Major Oggleton. He'd been a doctor and the mayor of Voorburg before the war. A good man. Quiet. But when he spoke up, he was so reasonable and calm that nobody could dispute him. He was a loss to the whole town."

"What happened to him?"

"He packed his bags one evening, took them to the train station, all spiffed up in his best suit and hat, got on a train, and was never seen or heard from again. As a medic, he'd seen the worst horrors of the war, and it destroyed him. For a little while before he left I'd lived next door to him, and I'd hear him wake up screaming in the middle of the night. I guess he thought he could leave the horrors behind in Voorburg. I doubt if it worked."

They sat in silence for a long moment. The tables had been cleared and the volunteers had gone away. The mess tent suddenly seemed the most depressing place on earth.

"Who was the third man you mentioned?" Jack asked finally.

"Captain VanZillen. We all looked up to him, though he was a hard man to really like. He was older than the rest of us. I think he was in insurance of some kind. A pretty high rank in his company, rich as hell, and he volunteered to leave his job to serve his country. Interesting man. Used to running things. Real good at money. Could calculate in his head like a wonder. He'd traveled a lot with his job and kept us going in the trenches with his stories of places he'd been and important people he'd met. It made us all feel good, thinking we'd go home and maybe someday see those places and people."

"Did he die as well?"

"Yes, but not on purpose like Butch and probably Major Oggleton. He was on some sort of trip on business when he got back." He stopped and thought for a moment. "I can't recall right off if it was a train or a ferry, but it went down crossing the Ohio River. Or maybe the Mississippi. Only four people out of about eighty managed to swim to shore. The rest were drowned and washed away. The river was high from rain, and turbulent, they said."

George smacked at an especially aggressive fly.

"I've told you the rumor that Hoover's going to throw us out of here tomorrow."

"Yes. But it's only a rumor, like you say." Then Jack asked, "Why did *you* come here?"

"Why not? Like I said, I haven't got a job and I've lost my family. All I have are my old buddies from the war. And at first I thought this march might work. But look what it's turned into." He pointed at two drunks rolling around in the dirt about twenty feet away, punching at each other fruitlessly.

Chapter 13

Howard Walker was having a peanut butter sandwich for a late lunch at his house by the river. He needed some quiet. Or at least as quiet as it got, next to Monday's usual influx of trains racing by. But he'd learned to tune them out pretty well.

He was waiting for more information before he could continue his investigation, so he used these few minutes of leisure to consider his investigators instead. Ralph Summer was strong and fairly obedient within his mental limits. He was good at guarding prisoners, not that there were ever many in Voorburg. Walker could give him the car keys, with directions for picking up a specific paper or piece of evidence, and he'd do it.

Ralph would act as he was told without any interest in what or why he was doing it. Ralph had no imagination, no ambition. Walker had inherited him from the former police chief, who'd been fired for incompetence and a general bad attitude. There wasn't enough in the town budget for another full-time deputy with brains. He could hire someone extra for a few days two or three times a year in emergencies, but that was it.

He longed to get rid of Ralph and hire Harry Harbinger, who was intelligent and hardworking. He also had that essential element, curiosity.

Unfortunately, it wasn't possible.

Ralph was badly equipped to get other work. Jobs weren't easy to find, and Ralph didn't make a good impression on strangers. For all his apparent outgoing and often boisterous bragging to his friends and acquaintances, he became shy with people he didn't know. And it was the type of shyness that seemed surly and uncooperative.

But the main reason he couldn't get rid of him was that Ralph and his cousin Jack were buying a house. This was no time to put a man out of a job he did fairly competently. Especially when he himself was the one who wanted to take over the premises where Ralph and Jack were currently living when they moved.

Howard couldn't finish the sandwich. It was such awful oily peanut butter. He shouldn't have scrimped and bought the cheapest he could find—and far too much of it. He went out on the porch, broke up the rest of the sandwich, and threw it out in the road. A mob of seagulls descended on it immediately.

Howard had to keep his deputy. Ralph wouldn't find anything else he was qualified to do. And maybe his lack of interest was a benefit. He didn't run off harebrained to investigate on his own. He could follow simple orders. He was stupid enough to do very dull work and not mind. And Harry Harbinger was good at scrambling in the pursuit of helping his family. He always had something to do. He was well liked, meticulous with every job he took on. Was able to charm people into thinking they needed something done. All told, Harry probably made more money doing odd jobs than the town paid the deputy.

Robert pulled up in the Duesie while Howard was still brooding.

"Thought I'd drop by and find out if we know anything more about the mummy," Robert said, making a circle around the seagulls polishing off Howard's sandwich.

"Mummy?" Howard said. His mind had been miles away. "I haven't even asked the guy in Albany."

"How come?"

"Robert, your mummy has been dead for years. I've got a murder that's only a day old. The mummy can wait a little longer. He won't care."

Robert grinned. "You've got a point." But Robert wasn't especially interested in Donald Anderson's death. He'd been generally disliked and wasn't liked any better dead. The mummified man fascinated him because it was a real puzzle. "Could I pretend to be your temporary deputy and call up to Albany myself?"

"Go ahead."

"How's the search for the satchel coming?"

"It's not. No sign of it. If it doesn't turn up today, I'm going to have to do something I don't want to."

"What's that?"

"Search the Anderson house."

"Why?" Robert objected. "Mrs. Anderson's the one who brought up his always carrying the satchel, even though everyone in town had seen him with it every day. Even if she was involved in his death, wouldn't she have disposed of it by now?"

That's why I'm giving her another day, Howard thought privately. He just shrugged. "We may still find it in the woods."

"What's Doc Polhemus got to say?"

Walker waved Robert inside, where he'd been studying Polhemus's report.

"Not much," he said, skimming the document. "Middle-aged white man in relatively good health. Slight asthma. Evidence of broken tibia (left) in childhood and broken ring finger (right) sometime in his last seven to ten years.

"Immediate cause of death: severe horizontal blow to the left temple. No sign of what sort of weapon. Most likely an object both heavy, relatively smooth, approximately four inches in diameter (determined by skull damage distribution), and traveling at a high velocity. Shattered orbital cavity leading to extensive blood clotting in the left

side of the brain. Paralyzation with unconscious-
ness resulting in approximately five minutes,
death following close behind. Minor postmortem
abrasions on back, legs, back and right side of
head."

"Does that tell us he was murdered?" Robert
asked.

"Nope. But it confirms that he was dragged
from the site where he died. And it suggests a
hard blow to the head, not just falling onto something. He didn't die from anything that matches
the description of any weapon in the vicinity. At
least nothing we've found yet. Lily's theory of a
coal car dropping something on him doesn't jive
with the horizontal impact if Polhemus is right.
I'm obligated to treat it as a murder."

"So where do you go from here?" Robert asked.

"I ask a lot of Nosey Parker questions nobody's
going to want to answer and sift around in the
replies for a solution."

When Lily returned to Grace and Favor, she
found Mrs. Prinney nearly knee-deep in seed cat-
alogs and every single gardening book the town
library owned. They were all bristling with little
paper markers.

"You changed your mind?" Lily asked.

"No, I'm changing my product. Not until next
spring, but it's never too early to start. I'm going
to grow flowers."

"Flowers? Why?"

Mrs. Prinney put another scrap of paper in between the pages of the catalog she was currently studying and said girlishly, "I've given this a lot of thought. What businesses are thriving around here?" She ticked them off on her fingers. "The movie house. The hairdresser. That man who travels around the local towns giving bridge lessons is making a fortune. And I hear that some floundering local businessmen are going to put their remaining cash into one of those miniature golf courses that are all the rage. Now, Lily dear, what do these have in common?"

Lily thought for a few moments and then grinned. "They're not necessary to living. Just pure enjoyment."

Mrs. Prinney nodded smugly, her chins jiggling. "That's right. And flowers make people happy. I've already got a garden plot to grow them in. I don't need to rent a building or hire help. I don't need to clear a big piece of land and buy lots of fancy gadgets. I don't have to travel around the countryside giving lessons. I'll make myself useful and other people happy. And do you know? There are flowers you can cook with. Not just the herbs and spices but actual flowers. It's perfect for me."

"It's going to be as much work as the vegetables, though, isn't it?"

"Not if a lot of them are long-flowering perennials. If you cut off the flowers of delphiniums, for example, when they're in their prime in the

spring, they'll bloom again in the fall. Not so glo-
riously, but they will bloom. I'd never have
known that without these books. And there are
lots of perennials that don't reach their peak until
autumn, when all the annuals are pretty ragged."

Lily knew what delphiniums were—that is, she
could recognize them in an arrangement. But she
had no idea what perennials were. Back in the
days when they were rich, her mother always had
the house, whichever one of five or six they were
living in, full of flower bowls and vases. She suspected her mother knew as little as she herself did
about how they grew, just asked the butler to
order them from whatever florist was closest.

But if Mrs. Prinney had her way—which was
inevitable—Lily would soon know more about
growing flowers than she ever wanted to. The
older woman wasn't shy about discussing her en-
thusiasms.

It took nearly half an hour of listening to Mrs.
Prinney convincing herself about her newest
project before Lily could manage a change of subject. When Mrs. Prinney finally ran down, Lily
asked, "Did you know Donald Anderson well?"

"I hardly knew him at all," Mrs. Prinney said.
"He was never in town much. He was a salesman
of some sort of equipment, they said, always traveling around the state. Then, when he lost his job,
he was still gone most of the time, doing odd jobs,
his wife told me. I feel so sorry for Roxanne. A
woman with children needs a man around."

"But she still has one. Her brother Eugene lives with them, I understand."

"Does he? That's odd. I thought he was only visiting for a while." She tilted her head, frowned, and said, "He's been there since last summer, come to think of it. I hope he sticks around to give his sister a hand. She's going to need all the help she can get."

Lily was inclined to a different view, but she didn't express it. It seemed to her from what she'd heard that Donald Anderson hadn't been much help to his wife for a long time. Even Roxanne admitted that the children had become wary of him and his bad moods. And he certainly wasn't true to his marriage vows, from what Ruby and Phoebe said, and she had no reason to disbelieve them. She was reluctant to discuss this aspect of his life with Mrs. Prinney for fear that Mrs. P. would see it as spreading nasty gossip. And maybe that's all it was. Or maybe he only made "inappropriate" remarks and gestures when he was drunk—not that that excused his behavior.

She wondered if Howard Walker knew what kind of man Donald Anderson had been. And whether she should tell him what she'd heard.

Chapter 14

Tuesday morning, Mrs. Prinney asked Lily, "Do you know how to drive the Duesenberg?"

"I know how to drive, but I've never driven the Duesie. Robert would have a fit if I tried to put my hand to the wheel."

"Is he busy today?"

"I don't think so. Why?"

"I want to go upriver a ways. I read last night in one of the gardening books that perennials should be planted in the fall so they have plenty of time over the winter to get rooted and set their blooms. I've heard several of the mansions up north have beautiful gardens. People go miles and miles to see them. And some of the places sell their extra plants to help pay the gardeners for keeping the garden going."

"But it's not fall yet. It's only the end of July."

"Still, I'd like to look over what I will want."

"I'll put it to Robert under one condition," Lily

said. "Tell me what perennials are without laughing at me."

"I thought you knew, dear. They're plants that
come back by themselves every year. You don't
have to grow them from seeds unless you want
to. And most of them, my books say, grow well
enough to divide with a shovel and have more
and more over the years."

Lily lifted an eyebrow. "You're thinking of
making Grace and Favor into one of those garden
showplaces, aren't you?"

"Why ever would you say that," Mrs. Prinney
said, gasping and blushing scarlet.

Lily smiled. "I'll ask Robert to drive us."

She ran into Mimi, their one maid, dusting the
furniture in the entry hall. She had her exces-
sively blond hair tied up in a red polka-dot scarf
and was sweating copiously as she crawled
under furniture to make sure she hadn't missed a
single speck. She still looked glamorous.

Lily bent down. "Have you any idea where
Robert is?"

"Yes, miss. He's in the library playing soli-
taire," Mimi replied, getting to her feet.

"Mrs. Prinney wants him to drive us to see
some flower gardens," Lily explained.

Mimi clasped her duster to her bosom. "Oh,
miss! I love flower gardens."

"Would you like to come along?"

Mimi frowned. "I've got the dusting to do. I always do the whole place on Tuesdays."

"Dusting can wait. It won't get any worse by tomorrow."

"I'd like to go *ever* so much," Mimi admitted. "May I put on clean clothes? I'll really hurry."

Lily was starting to think maybe Mrs. Prinney was right. In these hard times, people liked things that were beautiful or simply fun to do. Women especially liked to be pretty and have pretty things around them. Lily herself had put herself to sleep the night before thinking about her mother's various homes, awash in bowls and vases of colorful scented flowers, and wishing to be surrounded with them again. They would remind her of her mother.

The trip was soon arranged. Robert was at his wits' end with boredom. He wasn't allowed to finish tearing down the old icehouse until Walker said he could. He'd been unable to reach the pathologist in Albany. And any excuse to swan around in the Duesie appealed to him.

Lily sat in front with Robert. In the back, Mrs. Prinney gabbled to Mimi as they went along about plumbago, irises, dead nettle (which alarmed Robert), phlox, spirea bushes, larkspur, eucalyptus, peonies, roses, gladiolus, ferns, and chrysanthemums.

Tuesday seemed to Jack Summer to be the hottest, smelliest day he could ever remember experiencing. As the temperature climbed, the odors of the camp became more horrific, the flies more frantic, the children crankier, the men more sullen, the women more downtrodden and tending to weep at the slightest thing. He watched helplessly as a broken coffee cup reduced one old woman to complete hysteria.

"General" Walter Waters visited the camp later in the morning, making angry speeches. "Are you men or dogs? Will you cringe and yelp while your masters beat you?" Anyone looking as if they were packing up to go home was open to attack. He struck one man who was loading a wagon. "You're an enemy to the men who lost their lives in the Great War! A coward! Scum of the earth!" he shouted.

The man's little boy pushed at him. "Don't you talk ugly to my daddy!"

Waters shoved the child, and he fell down in a heap of horse manure. The mother of the child had to be restrained from going after Waters with a kitchen knife. Waters's khaki-clad bodyguards tried to haul her away to God knows where, and a fight broke out between the bodyguards and a dozen desperately discouraged and angry men.

Jack was disgusted. This Waters man who had posed as the savior of the maltreated veterans was now so out of control he was attacking children. Jack couldn't imagine anyone in the federal administration who even would say in private with his cronies such nasty things about the Bonus Army Marchers, much less saying it *to* them en masse.

As Waters returned to the city, there was a muted, ghostly chorus of boos following him. Other fistfights broke out between Waters's supporters and his critics.

Jack went in search of other men from Voorburg. But once again he discovered how hard it was to locate them, much less interview them. One was getting some well-deserved sleep. Another was helping a friend repair his refrigerator-crate home away from home. A third man Jack was seeking had gone over the bridge to the city to check out the latest rumors.

All over the camp, people were saying that the President had given the marchers this date as the day they must go home. A few, including Mary Towerton, were taking it seriously. When Jack got back to the tent, she was putting the children's clothing and her own in boxes while her grandfather berated her. "You silly girl! You can just go on home if you want, but I'm staying here!"

"No, you're not, Grampa. You're getting weaker and weaker, and I don't want to tote you home in a coffin."

"Is Grampa going to die?" her little boy asked.

"No, he's going to cooperate and take good care of himself." She seemed sorry the child had overheard her.

"No chit of a girl is going to tell me what to do!" Joe Wyman bellowed. The baby, startled out of fitful sleep, started screaming. Mary put her hands over her face and took a couple of deep breaths. She looked up at Jack then and said, "I've got everything ready. If you could put these last boxes in the cart, I'll get Grampa moving. Do you know how to hitch up a mule?"

"Nope. I've got a policy of staying away from mules," he said, trying to sound cheerful for her sake. "You hitch up the mule while I get some guys to manhandle your grandfather into the cart."

He grabbed a couple of relatively friendly strangers who were lounging around and explained that a young woman with two children needed help with her grandfather.

"It's something to do," one said.

The old man used up all his strength and invective trying to resist, but eventually the younger, stronger men prevailed. They were surprisingly gentle with the old man, who kept trying to hit them with his cane.

"Do you know how to get home?" Jack asked Mary.

"I got us here. I can get us back," she said grimly. Then she forced herself to smile. "Thank you, Mr. Summer. I couldn't have done this without your help."

Joe Wyman, spread-eagled in the back of the wagon, was already snoring like the devil as his granddaughter urged the mule toward the Eleventh Street Bridge.

Jack went back inside the tent. He was glad to be rid of old Joe, but he would miss Mary. He lay down on the dirt floor, using his small suitcase as a pillow, and thought he might get some sleep at last.

But it wasn't to be. Within ten minutes there was an uproar outside. People were shouting, running all over.

"What's happening?" He grabbed one man's arm to stop him.

Struggling to get away, the man said hurriedly, "Hoover's got the police and army throwing everyone out of the government buildings in the city. They've got tanks and sabers and are tear-gassing people. Everybody's rushing to the aid of the vets."

He shook off Jack's grasp and headed toward the bridge.

The United States Army was attacking the veterans of the previous generation?

Jack gasped. Could this possibly be true? Suddenly he realized that Mary Towerton and her children and grandfather were inadvertently part of the exodus of overwrought, angry men. He started running to catch up with her. He'd help her turn the wagon back and tell her to go north through Maryland and circle around the city to escape. He just hoped he could do this and still get back in time to find out what, if anything, was really happening.

He started running with the rest, being jostled and pushed just as he was rudely pushing past anyone slower than himself. He was almost to the

bridge when he spotted the ears of a mule over
the crowd. When he got closer he could see that it
was Mary's cart, stopped in the road. The mule
had his ears back and was braying and snorting
and starting to buck. The cart was rocked by men
trying to get around and even under it. Mary
looked terrified.

Jack climbed up beside her. "There's a rumor
that police and troops are putting men out in the
streets in the city. We have to get turned around
and go the other way."

Mary gazed with horror at the tide of people
behind them. "We'll both have to steady the
mule," she said, in a remarkably sensible voice.

He helped her down from the cart after she'd se-
cured the baby in its cot in the back and warned
her older child on pain of death *not* to get out of the
wagon. She and Jack went to gentle the mule and
Mary said quietly, while she patted the animal, "I
think Grampa is dead. He's not snoring anymore."

"If that's so, we can't do anything but get you
and the children out of here. Let's lead the mule
to the right side of the road and try to get turned
around."

They kept trying to get to the right, but it took
a long time. As they were forced closer and closer
to the bridge, Jack could see that the crowd was
stopping. He stood up on the seat of the wagon,
barely able to keep his balance long enough to see
that the bridge was barricaded by three tanks
with turret guns aimed at the oncomers.

When they finally got to the right of the road, Jack said, "Get down in the back and hold tight to the children."

As Mary did as she was told, Jack discovered there was a whip in a metal holder at his side. It hadn't been used for so long it was almost rusted in place. He wrenched it loose, pulled violently on the right rein, and smacked the rump of the mule with the whip as hard as he could.

Chapter 15

The gardening expedition visited several fine gardens. At the last one, the house looked a bit sad and shabby, but the gardens were spectacular. This, they assumed, was the mansion most likely to sell plants. Robert strolled off and found the head gardener and with effusive compliments and the exchange of very little money made a deal that would allow Mrs. Prinney to take home a few perennials. "Just to get her started," Robert told the gardener.

Mrs. Prinney purchased for Grace and Favor two substantial bushel baskets of cuttings and seedlings wrapped in damp newspapers. Mimi had been assigned to write down the names and stick them with the right items. Lily had merely roamed around, gawking and thinking how very pretty everything was. There were little islands of colorful things edged with what Mrs. Prinney said was boxwood. Lily had spotted the gardener trimming it to boxlike perfection with nail scissors.

On the way back, they had to stop twice to get a glass of water to refresh the little seedlings. On the second stop—at a gasoline station—Mrs. Prinney met with resistance, and while she negotiated with the owner, Robert, who was still thinking about his mummy, said to Lily, "I wish there was someone who knew when the icehouse in the woods was abandoned."

Mimi, in the backseat, filing her nails intently, said, "Nineteen twenty-six."

Robert's head snapped around. "Are you sure of that?"

Mimi nodded, holding out her hand to see if her nails were all even lengths. "It was the year Miss Flora, your great-uncle Horatio's aunt, died. Her father had had the icehouse in the woods built years before, I think. But the butler was nearly as old as Miss Flora was, and he put his big ol' foot down and said he wasn't going clear into the woods to get the ice no more."

Robert had to resist slapping his head for his stupidity. He should have realized long ago that Mimi would know the most about the history of Grace and Favor. Her mother had been housekeeper and nurse for Miss Flora when Mimi was a child, and when Mimi's mother died, Mimi herself took over until the old woman's death. When Robert and Lily's great-uncle, Horatio Brewster, moved into the house he brought his own staff and let Mimi and the butler go.

Mrs. Prinney came back to the Duesie with her glass of water.

"Isn't that going to make the ink run on the labels?" Lily said.

Mimi had put away her nail file and was helping Mrs. Prinney move the seedlings around so they all got a drink. "No, I did them in pencil."

"Robert, we must hurry home," Mrs. Prinney said, after returning the glass to the proprietor. "I don't want them to dry out. I don't suppose you'd be willing to put your jacket over them lightly?"

"No, I wouldn't," Robert said in a remarkably gentle tone.

He was worried about what the floor of the Duesie was going to look like with all that dirty water. And he was in a hurry as well. He wanted to get home and have a further conversation with Mimi about the icehouse's history.

Jack got Mary and the Towerton children out into the countryside. He kept glancing back at Joe. The old man's lips were blue. Mary was right about him being dead. They were part of a long cortege of other vehicles fleeing to Baltimore. But it was slightly more orderly than the rush to Washington had been.

As they approached a small town about three miles away, Jack spoke quietly to Mary. "You have to bury him here."

Mary put her hands to her cheeks. "I can't do

that," she whispered. "He wanted to be buried on his own land."

"Mrs. Towerton, be sensible. It's a long way home and very hot. He'll start to"—Jack was about to say "stink" but altered the phrase—"disintegrate pretty soon. You don't want to do that to your children. Bury him here. And when times get better you can have him moved home."

Jack found the furniture and coffin maker and gave Mary all his money to pay for the coffin. He had his return train ticket and hadn't spent the extra on a hotel. He could beg or borrow enough to get a meal or two on his way back to Voorburg. And if he couldn't, it didn't matter if he got hungry. Mary needed to bury her grampa. Soon. But would the money be enough to bury him decently? Jack wondered. Would it pay for grave diggers, let alone a marker of some kind?

They took a short walk with the children while the undertaker and his assistant removed old Joe from the cart. Jack left Mary and her children sitting on a bench in front of the shop and started greeting others who were passing through in their frantic flight from their own government. He explained that a young mother of two little children was leaving Anacostia Flats when her grandfather died on the journey. He pleaded with strangers to contribute what they could. When he returned to fetch Mary, he had another nine dollars and thirty-seven cents that he turned over to her. They went back to the cart.

"Where's Grampa?" Mary's little boy asked.

Mary bent down to him, "He's going to stay here and visit a friend for a few days. We're going home now."

She turned to Jack and shook his hand. "I'll pay you back somehow. I'll never forget your help."

Jack said, "I'll see you in Voorburg soon. You know the way from here?"

She said, "That's the way we came down here. I remember the route." Then Jack took off at a dogtrot to go back to the Anacostia Flats. He was still a reporter.

Robert had cornered Mimi privately when they got back to Grace and Favor and said, "Tell me everything you remember about the old icehouse."

Mimi explained that Miss Flora had died at the start of 1926. The icehouse had been abandoned for a couple of months by then. When Mr. Horatio came to live at Grace and Favor a month later, the icehouse still had a key in the door, but it wasn't locked.

"I'd grown girl to woman in the mansion," she said, "and I surely missed it. Sometimes I'd walk clear up here from town and just sit and look at it from the woods."

"Was the icehouse still unlocked that summer?"

"I think so. I remember peeking inside. It was a spooky ol' place, all dark and dry. At Christmastime, I got lonely. I went back up to see the mansion and noticed that the key to the icehouse was gone. I tried the door, but it wouldn't budge."

"So, sometime between February and December of 1926 somebody locked it up?"

"That's right."

"Did you ever go back to see if it was open again?"

Mimi looked at him. "Why would I do that? I didn't like the place. I was glad it was locked up. I really didn't want to scare myself again."

"Did you notice anything else?"

"Like what?"

"Scuff marks around the door?" Robert asked. "Broken plants? Anything strange?"

"Nothing but that the door was locked," Mimi replied. "I gotta catch up with my dusting, Mr. Robert."

When Jack returned to camp to see if he could find his suitcase, he was horrified. The place was in flames. There were tanks, and soldiers with sabers setting fire to everything. Those marchers who had stayed behind were being brutally thrown out of their pitiful structures, not even allowed to gather their belongings. Men, women, and children were coughing from the smoke, vomiting, and squinting, their red eyes streaming in the gas-laden air.

Jack was disoriented and couldn't find the Towertons' tent. He wrapped his handkerchief around his nose and mouth and kept searching.

He ran into George Newman, the former teacher he'd spoken to earlier. He hardly recognized the man at first with all the soot on his face. "Who's doing this?" Jack demanded.

"President Hoover has sent his dogs of war," George said, with a disgusted sneer. "General MacArthur and his aide, Major Eisenhower, are in charge. And that son of a bitch Patton's around somewhere with his cavalry, running down as many people as he can reach."

"I'm lost," Jack admitted. "I need my suitcase. My notes are in it. Is Joe's tent still standing?"

"Last time I saw, it was. Over there."

Jack went the way George had pointed and found the tent in flames. He *had* to get his notes. Taking a deep breath and holding his arms over his head, he ran inside, grabbed his case and tore back out. When he was safely out of the tent, he put the case between his feet and started slapping his hair and clothes where sparks were burning.

As he did so, a child across the way headed for a tar-paper shack that soldiers were also approaching. "Mister," the boy said to one of the soldiers, "I gotta get my pet rabbit, please."

The soldier said, "Get the hell outa here, you little bastard," and prodded the child's leg with his bayonet.

A man appeared, shoving through the horrified crowd, and scooped the child up, holding one hand over the little scrawny leg, which was bleeding copiously.

"Johnny, we'll get you another rabbit," he said, running, coughing, and trying to stuff the little boy's face into his shirt to protect him from the smoke.

The first anyone at home knew about this was when Lily turned on the radio late that evening. It had been so hot in her room that even Agatha couldn't sleep. Lily and the dog crept downstairs, opened the library windows, and turned on a fan to catch whatever breeze might blow up from the river. Sitting in the dark, Lily thought some soothing music might help her go to sleep. She switched on the massive radio and started turning the dial for music but caught a semihysterical voice. ". . . in Washington and on the Anacostia Flats. Fires leap so high and fiercely that the White House itself is bathed in orange light. . . ."

Lily jumped to her feet, ran upstairs, and pounded on Robert's bedroom door.

"What's wrong!" he said, his hair tousled and sweaty and his eyes bleary.

"Come down and listen to the radio. There are apparently huge fires burning somewhere near Washington."

Robert threw on a dressing gown and raced downstairs.

". . . and (*cough*) there's so much tear gas in the (*cough*) air, I'm going to have to close down this connection."

The radio was alarmingly quiet for a few moments, and then an announcer came on. "We hope our reporter can get back to us soon. As you heard him say, the U.S. Army attacked the Bonus Marchers in Washington this afternoon. They evicted those occupying abandoned government buildings at gun- and saber-point and with tear gas. Tanks moved down and crossed the Eleventh Street Bridge, pushing the crowd of marchers and local people before them. The camp on the Anacostia Flats is now in flames. So far we have no news of fatalities. We'll interrupt this program if new information comes to us from Washington."

The soothing music Lily had sought earlier commenced.

"Dear God!" Lily said. "Jack's there somewhere."

Robert was leaning forward, elbows on knees. "Sometimes the newspeople get things wrong. But this sounded real. How on earth could Hoover do this to American citizens? The heroes of the Great War?"

Chapter 16

Robert went to Poughkeepsie early in the morning to get all the New York City papers the moment they were delivered and brought them back. Editorials screamed.

"What a pitiful spectacle, the great American Government chasing unarmed men, women, and children with army tanks."

"If the United States Army must be called out to make war on unarmed citizens, this is no longer America."

The Hoover administration saw to it that the few newspapers still favorable to him editorialized that the Bonus Army was composed of criminals and Communists who had taken advantage of the true veterans.

General MacArthur was quoted as saying, "I have released in my day more than one community which had been held in the grip of a foreign enemy." He didn't specify what foreign enemy he was referring to this time.

President Hoover himself informed the press that "A challenge to the authority of the United States Government has been met, swiftly and firmly."

Other news programs said definitively that Hoover had given MacArthur specific warnings not to cross the Eleventh Street Bridge, an order from his commander in chief that MacArthur treasonably ignored. Other sources of news emphatically denied that this was true.

The whole household of Grace and Favor and most of the rest of Voorburg were glued to the radio all the next day. Reports conflicted. One said only two marchers had been killed, another said over fifty veterans had been massacred in cold blood in front of their wives and children. A Negro infant in a Washington neighborhood had died of suffocation from tear gas. Men on the Anacostia Flats had had their ears cut off with army sabers.

The only common thread was that the march was well and truly over.

Everyone had scattered. Some were heading for New York City to occupy Central Park. Others had gone to Johnstown, Pennsylvania, where they were heartily welcomed by the mayor. Many had fled to Camp Bartlett, just over the Maryland state line, a thirty-acre site that had been donated by a former Republican governor for the overflow of marchers. Many marchers' families had firmly believed they'd prevail and had left homes they couldn't go back to, out of shame or because they'd sold them before leaving for Washington.

A few people in Voorburg, however, weren't reading newspapers or listening to the news. Chief of Police Howard Walker and his deputy, Ralph Summer, were on their way to the Anderson home.

"I'm sorry, Mrs. Anderson," Walker said at the door, "I have a warrant to search your house."

Roxanne, who had opened the front door a mere three inches, turned and said to her brother, "Don't say a word. I've done nothing wrong." Looking back at Walker, she went on, haughtily, "Look all you want. Eugene and I will take the children outside in the backyard so they don't see what shame you're putting on our family."

"I regret this as much as you do," Walker admitted. Ralph rolled his eyes in astonishment.

"No. You don't," Roxanne said, closing but not latching the door.

Ralph pushed the door back open and Walker snatched the deputy by the elbow. "*I* say when we go in."

Ralph looked about half as surly as Walker.

They waited until they heard the children playing in the yard. Walker warned Ralph for the third time this morning, "If you find anything suspicious, don't touch it. Just tell me about it.

You search upstairs, I'll search the ground floor, and then we'll both do the outbuildings."

Walker started in the main front room. He found nothing hidden but homemade children's toys that had slipped down between cushions or under skirted chairs. He examined the fireplace very carefully. The ashes were cold and dry and nothing had been burned for months. He'd started looking through the china cabinet in the dining room when Ralph came pounding down the stairs clutching a satchel to his chest with both big clumsy hands across its front. "Hey, Chief, look what I found."

"Ralph, you donkey's ass! How many times did I tell you not to touch anything? Damn you, put it down. And don't ever call me chief again, you fool." It was all Howard could do to prevent himself from beating Ralph to a pulp.

"Sorry . . . *Chief* Walker," Ralph said, with what he thought was clever sarcasm.

Walker had brought along a fresh cardboard box lined with white paper to carry away anything suspicious. He picked up the satchel by the corner with a piece of the paper over his hand and laid it gently in the box. Ralph had probably smeared his own fingerprints and fibers from his shirt all over the satchel already.

"Where'd you find this?" His voice was almost shaking with anger. At Ralph. And himself.

"Under a bed with one of those skirt things around it."

"Show me where. And for God's sake, don't touch anything else or I'll tie your hands behind your back and thrash you within an inch of your life."

"What are you so grumpy about?"

"You, Ralph. You!"

Ralph clomped angrily up the stairs and pointed to a doorway. "In there."

It was the main bedroom. The furniture was once good, but was shabby now. There was a large bed between the two windows facing the hill behind, covered by a lightweight summer quilt in tiny squares of yellow and green. It was neatly made. A yellow gathered fabric hung to the floor beneath the quilt. A rocking chair in the corner of the room had the same quilting and ruffle on the cushion.

Walker leaned down carefully and lifted the ruffle, shining a flashlight under the bed. It was dusty, but there was a partially clear area where Ralph had dragged out the satchel on the far side. Another baby doll had found its way there, as well, and a dusty little wooden truck with a string to pull it.

He realized that the surfaces of the house that would be seen by visitors had been cleaned, but the other parts hadn't. That's what happened, he supposed, when good housewives had to work so much harder than they had had to before 1929.

He carefully examined the rest of the room. He checked drawers in the tall chest, respectfully lifting neat piles of clothing to see if something was hidden under them. Mrs. Anderson's nightwear was old-fashioned and carefully patched. So were Donald's underwear and the freshly laundered and rather stiffly ironed dresses in the looming wardrobe. Two outworn old men's suits hung at the other end of the rod. Some plaid shirts and work trousers of Donald's were laid across the top of a treadle sewing machine in the corner. Apparently Roxanne, now a widow, was planning to use the fabric to make clothes for her children out of them. A few framed ancestors, stony-faced and grim, stared down from the top of the wardrobe with disapproval.

The center of the room had a blue hooked rug, thin and flat from long wear, but Walker still pulled it up around all the edges. He found nothing but a brass hairpin.

Ralph had stood the whole time in the doorway, rocking gently back and forth and only moving his eyes to watch his boss. "Nothing else, huh?"

Walker didn't answer. He just brushed past Ralph to look over the other two bedrooms. One was a tiny guest room, apparently occupied by Eugene and his child: a single high bed and a smaller one on rollers that apparently could be put under the high one. A washstand and a towel bar matched a pitcher for water at the edge of the sink, with a small yellow bar of soap and a small square mirror for shaving. There wasn't even room for a rug on the floor.

At the other end of the hallway was another large bedroom with three beds very close together and a toy box, bookshelf, and single nightstand with a lamp shared by two of the beds. A very small bathroom had been recently installed between the two larger bedrooms, probably the last improvement to the house before money and jobs were in short supply.

Walker went back downstairs and thoroughly examined the kitchen as well. A big badly dented table filled the center of the room, and half a dozen mismatched wooden chairs were around it. A small icebox. A fairly new range, spotlessly clean. A pantry behind a wide white door. Walker looked through everything and found nothing unusual. The pantry was sparsely supplied with flour in colorful cotton bags, home-canned vegetables, and baskets of fresh vegetables from Roxanne's garden. A canning steamer and empty bottles were on a top shelf, along with the necessary tongs, funnels, and dishcloths. An old telephone was on the wall of the kitchen. He picked up the handset; there was no sound. Mrs. Anderson had told them the service had been cut off.

He went to the back door and looked out the window. Mrs. Anderson was standing next to it. He tapped lightly. She opened the door.

"We need to look in the garage and shed."

"I'll take the children out front. I presume you didn't find anything."

"Your husband's satchel," Walker said.

Roxanne, who had been half turned away, spun around to face him. "Where?"

"Under your bed."

"What? No!"

"We'll talk about it later," Walker said. Mrs. Anderson's face had become so white he was half afraid she was going to faint. But she pulled herself together and herded the children away.

There was an old Ford on blocks in the garage, probably because the Andersons could no longer afford gas. Oily rags and a length of thin rope to hang clothes to dry were on hooks on the wall. Enormous tin buckets to wash and rinse the clothes were against the far wall. The shed held gardening tools and watering cans and had a high shelf with empty seed packets.

Walker and Ralph went to the front of the house. "Might I have a private word with you, Mrs. Anderson?" Walker said.

Eugene stepped forward. "I don't think my sister should talk to you. She's very upset."

"I think everyone is upset, but I have to speak to her here or take her to town. I'd rather it was here, and I think she might feel that way as well."

Roxanne put her hand on her brother's arm. "Don't worry, Gene. I'm all right. I'm not the sort to run around admitting anything that's not true. And I have absolutely nothing to conceal."

He looked at her for a long while before saying, "I'll take the kids inside and give them some of those cookies you made this morning."

"He'll spoil their lunch," she said under her breath, then shrugged and faced Walker with fire in her eyes.

Chapter 17

Roxanne sat down on the top step of the front porch and indicated that Howard Walker should sit next to her. She was almost smiling but not quite.

In a voice as delicate and deadly as a rapier, she said, "Chief Walker, I'm a smart, hardworking, commonsense woman. Ask anyone you like if this isn't true. I know I'm your best suspect in my husband's murder, but can you really imagine I'm stupid enough to implicate myself by hiding that satchel under my own bed?"

"Can you explain it, then?"

"No. And I don't have to," she said. "But I'll tell you what I do know. Donald left Saturday morning when I was in the bathtub. I always lock the door to keep the children out. It's the only time I ever have alone. He called goodbye through the door.

"I didn't see him," she went on. "I didn't know

what he was wearing. I didn't know where he
was going. I didn't know whether he had the
satchel with him. Occasionally when he had a
dirty job that lasted a couple of days, he wore his
work clothes instead of his suit."

"But he was wearing a suit when he was
found."

She put out her hands in a so-what gesture. "I
didn't know that when you told me he'd died.
For all I knew, he was doing some sort of office
work and didn't need his work clothes and left
the satchel behind. I haven't had time or energy
to dust under that bed for months, let alone pull
up the skirt to see what's under it."

"He didn't tell you where he was working?"

"He usually didn't know. He just went looking
for any job he could get. I'll swear to all this and
so will my brother. Most of the town knows our
situation as well. Question anyone you wish
about my standards and morals. I've lived here
all my life in this very house. It was my parents'
and my mother's parents' before her."

"I don't doubt I'd get a good report from
everyone," Howard said. "But I can't even explain to myself, much less anyone else, how the
satchel he was known to carry almost every day
ended up under the bed."

"I don't know either. That's the dad-blamed
truth, and you can believe it or not. I did *not* kill
my husband."

Howard was quiet for a while. "Suppose he

had the satchel with him?" She started to say something and he held up a hand to stop her. "Just suppose. Could the person who killed him have come in your house and hidden it there to suggest that you'd done it?"

She thought a moment. "Frankly, it's unlikely. But possible. Since I learned of his death, a great many neighbors have been in and out of the house. I keep finding casseroles sitting on the kitchen table when we come inside. We don't have locks on the doors. We all spend a lot of time outside. My brother and my children all help in the garden."

"You've been gardening these last few days?"

She looked at him as if he were mad. "Of *course* we have. Our lives can't stop. We need the money we make on the vegetables. There's weeding and watering to be done every day so I can produce the best and freshest food of anyone in town."

"Do you miss your husband?" Walker hadn't really meant to ask this. It just came into his mind and out his mouth before he could think about it.

She answered immediately. "No. You might as well know from me before someone else tells you, if they haven't already. Donald wasn't a good husband, not for a long time. Even before he lost his job, he was having flings with other women, and it only got worse after the Crash."

"You didn't care?"

"I cared horribly at first. It was such a betrayal of my trust. I'd really loved him when we married, and for a long time after. But I was smarter and harder-working than he was, and he didn't like it. He wanted women he had no obligation to. Women who were prettier and more docile than I, which is almost anyone. Women who have lots of time on their hands to pamper a man, make fancy desserts, wear nightgowns I'd look silly in, as tall and angular as I am."

Howard looked down at her work-toughened hands for a moment, wondering how honest she could be if pressed harder. He said, "I admit I've heard gossip about your husband and other women. But do you have proof of it? Did you ever follow him to find out for sure?"

Roxanne leaned back and gave him a half-amused look. "When a man can't stand to stay home, has good old school friends in other towns he visits, and his wife is never invited along or even introduced to them, a wife *knows*. It's not male friends or couples in spite of what he pretends when he comes home smelling of perfume. It's a woman or a string of women he's spending his time with."

"Did you ever confront him over this? Did you ask who he was really visiting?"

She sat back up, very straight. "A couple of times. But he lied. Indignantly. He was a very bad liar. He gave himself away with his pretended outrage."

Howard looked her straight in the eye. "Why didn't you divorce him?"

"I've never talked about this to anyone. And if I weren't a suspect I wouldn't be telling you, of all people. I didn't divorce him because nobody in my family has ever been divorced. I'd have lost some of my family and friends' respect. Even my dead relatives would have haunted me," she added with a fleeting smile.

She stood up slowly, preparing to finish this conversation and dismiss him.

"But it was mainly because I had a memory of him when he was young and I believed he was honorable. I still think he was once a good man. He was a good father. He was once charming and funny. Maybe he still was with other people, for all I know. I kept hoping that, when things got better, he might turn back into the man I married."

She crossed her well-tanned arms in a defensive way.

"I wasn't really stupid enough to believe it, but I wanted to."

Howard stood as well. "I have only one more question for you today. If you've known all along how much he'd betrayed you, why did you react as you did when I told you he was dead?"

She looked down for a moment and said softly, "Because once or twice I'd wished that he'd run out on us, as so many other men have. And I was afraid God had listened to me at the wrong time and taken it too far."

Fearing she might cry, Walker fumbled for a handkerchief, but she looked up at him, perfectly dry-eyed.

"I've never opened my heart and told anyone this. And I hope you don't need to tell anyone else my secret humiliations. But now you know, and I hope to heaven that you'll leave us alone to get on with our lives in peace."

"I can't promise that."

Her expression hardened. "All I can say is that I didn't kill my husband. I swear this on my mother's grave. And I don't know who did. I'm not sure I ever want to know. But I've told you the truth. There are certainly lots of other people who might have wanted him dead. Probably the husbands of some of his women. Now, will you please leave?"

Howard nodded, considered shaking her hand and rejected the idea, and went back to the car. Ralph was taking a nap and barely stirred when he started the engine.

He believed she'd told the truth. Maybe not the whole truth, but an awful lot of her own pain had been laid in his hands. She really was a remarkably strong-minded, sensible woman. He could genuinely admire her, but he wasn't sure every man in town would enjoy being married to someone like her. If a man didn't have the ambition, common sense, and honesty of a woman like

Mrs. Anderson, marriage with her might be absolute hell.

Jack Summer had hooked himself up with a contingent of veterans who were headed for New York City. Those on foot were invited to ride in the automobiles and farm carts of the others. At least he still had his train ticket home, thank goodness. He would have had to walk or hitch rides clear to Voorburg if he hadn't rescued his suitcase. He was dirty, exhausted, deeply upset, and hungry as hell. His clothes and hair stank. He had burns on his arms and was still periodically having coughing fits. But so was everyone else. The chances of a respectable person giving him a lift would have been slim.

He kept hoping Mary Towerton had come the same way, and he'd overtake her. But he didn't see a woman with a wagon, mule, and children.

Fortunately, he discovered he had a little change in his suitcase, enough to get one really substantial meal. Instead, he spent the money on a new pencil and a fresh pad of paper and had just enough left for a cup of coffee and a doughnut before the train left. He waited for the 7 P.M. train because he didn't want to inflict himself on the crowds going home from work on the late-afternoon trains. He had his first column for the *Voorburg-on-Hudson Times* written by the time they passed Croton. Then he started on the next one.

In the back of his mind, however, was Mary Towerton. He wished he knew what her route home was. He felt an obligation to get one night's sleep and then go find her, to help her complete her journey with an adult along.

Chapter 18

Lily was up early, dressed and ready to hunt down Jack Summer. It had been another stifling hot night, and she'd fretted for sleepless hours over what had become of him. The reports of the rout of the Bonus Marchers were so frightening that she feared he was hurt, lost, having amnesia. Her imagination was running riot.

But Mrs. Prinney caught her at the door. "Oh, dear. I must have misunderstood," she said, sounding hurt.

"Misunderstood what?" Lily replied, looking around for where she'd put her handbag.

"I thought you said you'd help me put in these baby plants this morning while it's fairly cool."

Lily was starting to think she ought to start taking notes of what she'd committed to. Had she really made this promise? In a weak moment, she might have said something vague about helping. "The heat's gotten to my brain, I guess," she said apologetically. "I'll put on my dungarees and be out in a moment."

Escape wasn't granted her until almost noon. Although she had to admit that until the sun shifted to the partly shady area they'd worked in, putting in the cuttings had been a soothing, pleasant thing to do. She'd liked the smells of the foliage, the odor of the rich earth they turned, the scents of pine that occasionally drifted over them from the trees deep in the woods. It was nice to kneel in the cool grass, until the sunshine got to them and made everything steam. On a nicer day in spring or autumn, she might have liked it even more. Gardening might not be such a bad hobby.

She came inside and phoned Jack's office, but there was no answer. She showered, dressed again in a skirt and blouse, but realized she simply couldn't face the long walk down the road, and the path through the woods would be almost as bad in the heat of the day. Robert had gone somewhere and she was tired of asking him to drive her places. Jack Summer wasn't a child. Surely if he'd had some serious trouble he'd have found some way to alert them or at least call his cousin Ralph.

But she had her walking shoes on, so out of curiosity she went to find the old abandoned icehouse where Robert and the Harbinger boys had found the mummy. She'd never really explored the woods to the north of Grace and Favor, where Robert said it was. Probably there was an old path that would lead her to it.

She found Agatha sleeping soundly under some bushes where it was cool and damp and rousted her out. "If I can go for a walk in the heat, so can you," she told the dog, who took her up on the offer with bouncing, barking delight.

She felt safer exploring unknown territory with Agatha along. She had never felt in danger in the woods before, but, after all, Robert had found a dead body and there were getting to be more and more hoboes around. Agatha had once come to her defense when she was threatened and no doubt would do it again if necessary.

The icehouse was, as she'd hoped, reasonably easy to find. It wasn't visible from the mansion, but she could catch glimpses of Grace and Favor through the woods when she got there, so she could easily find her way back.

It was very sturdy indeed, made entirely of solid wood so tightly fitted she could see why it had been weatherproof. And it was much larger than she'd imagined, almost the size of a tiny one-room house. She wondered if it had once served some other purpose. A hideaway for hunters caught in bad weather? Maybe it was even a home at one time, and the windows had been boarded over. The woods were too thick and the vines too dense at the back to see if there had been a window there.

As she was coming back along the side, Agatha let out a low growl. Not a serious growl, more of a curious one. A twig snapped. A step later, Lily ran into the young man she'd seen in town with the violin case.

They both yelped with surprise and Agatha barked.

The carrier of the violin had shrieked in a distinctly feminine voice, Lily realized. And looking more closely, she saw there wasn't so much as a hint of a beard.

"You're a *girl*, aren't you?" Lily asked.

"Yes, ma'am," the girl said, taking off her cap and releasing shoulder-length dark hair.

"What are you doing here?"

"Just looking for a place for me and my friends to settle down in the shade and rest a bit. It's terribly hot, ma'am."

Three more girls dressed as boys crept out of the woods and joined her. "Trouble, Judy?" one asked loudly.

The girl looked at Lily for a moment and said, "I don't think so. You don't mind, do you, ma'am?"

All four were slim young women wearing baggy men's clothing. Nobody would have guessed the slender figures concealed by their trousers and big plaid shirts. None wore makeup. Two had very short hair almost like men; the other two, including the violin girl, wore boys' caps that concealed their hair. Only one looked distinctively feminine. They were all dirty and sweaty, and their clothing was almost in rags.

"I won't tell anyone you're here as long as you

don't steal and you tell me about yourselves. Bargain?" Lily asked.

"We ain't stole nothing from nobody!" the one who'd addressed the violin girl as Judy said belligerently.

"Cynthia," Judy warned, in a soft voice.

"If that's true," Lily said, "I can probably find you a little food. And some soap if you'd like it."

Their eyes lit up. Lily had no idea if it was the mention of the food or the soap that caused it. The violin girl, Judy, was apparently the spokeswoman, and rightly so. She was obviously well educated and had good manners. "That would be generous, ma'am. But why do you want to know about us?"

"Curiosity, I guess, Judy. My name's Lily, by the way. I can't imagine doing what you girls are doing. Or why. Think it over while my dog and I go back to our house. I'll come back in a few minutes. Agatha, stop smelling everyone's knees," she added. "Come with me!"

Lily felt she had to explain to Mrs. Prinney why she needed half a loaf of bread, some cheese and pickles, and a bar of her treasured rose-scented soap. To Lily's surprise, the older woman was willing to help out. "I feel so bad about those girls who are on the road. Imagine having no family except your girlfriends to rely on."

"Roxanne Anderson says they steal her vegetables," Lily felt honor bound to say.

Mrs. Prinney shook her head. "I don't know if

that's true. I wouldn't like to think so anyway. You go get your soap, Lily. Agatha, get your head out of that paper bag! Dogs don't eat lettuce."

When Lily returned to the kitchen, Mrs. Prinney had nearly filled the bag. Two loaves of bread. A half-dozen overripe plums. Three precious oranges. A spotlessly clean bottle of fresh water. Some clean rags to wash with, a head of lettuce. The last few slices of a ham and a little bottle of mustard and a butter knife to spread it.

"Bring back the bottle and the knife," she said, turning away and brusquely touching a handkerchief to her eyes. "When I think of these girls and then think of my own daughters, I thank God my own are well."

The hobo girls were thrilled with the treat and seemingly surprised that Lily returned at all. "Cynthia said you'd gone for the police," Judy said. "I told her she was wrong. You seem like a nice person. I'm usually good at knowing who's nice and who isn't."

"I can't take credit for anything but the soap," Lily admitted. "Like you, my brother and I have practically no money and no jobs. The woman we live with has four daughters not much older than you four, and it was she who gave you the food."

"You don't have money or a job?" Judy asked. "Why does this woman let you live with her and give away her food?"

"It's a long, boring story," Lily said. It was the first time she'd admitted to strangers that she and

Robert were poor, and it was something of a relief to actually speak the words. But she wasn't ready to go further with the complicated reason. "Tell me about yourselves."

One of the girls was making sandwiches of the bread and ham and slathering them generously with mustard. She handed one to Judy. Judy picked off a tiny bit of the ham and gave it to Agatha, who for once took food politely.

"My mother wanted me to have a way to support myself if I needed to. She'd been a classical violinist herself and made her own living before she married my father, and this"—she tapped on the violin case—"is hers. She played in a good orchestra when she was young. I had the best teachers and was supposed to go to music school, but my mother died of pneumonia and my dad lost his job. He wanted me to go work in one of the cotton mills down south where he came from. Wanted us to move to South Carolina where they make cloth."

"Did you run away instead?" Lily asked.

"No. I did what he said. He was my father and I was only just seventeen. We moved and he got me a job, but before the month was out, I nearly caught my hand in a piece of machinery. I lost only the nail on my little finger."

She held up her right hand to show Lily.

"Right then," she went on, "I knew I'd betray my mother's dreams if I hurt my hands. So I took to the road. Met up with other girls along the way and found a few musical ones. Cynthia plays a harmonica. She also plays a trumpet but doesn't have one now; she sold it for food. And Ellie sings wonderfully. We stand on sidewalks and make music, and sometimes a few people put coins in the box that's on the ground. Josephine isn't musical," she said, with a smile to the prettiest girl, "but she keeps an eye on the money."

"Couldn't you get a job at a theater or movie house? Or even a speakeasy?" Lily asked.

"We was offered one," Cynthia said, her temper mellowing considerably, now that she had a sandwich inside of her. "But they wanted us to dress up and we couldn't afford to buy clothes."

Lily was thinking of all the fancy dresses she'd brought to Grace and Favor in one of her trunks that no longer fit her or were in style. Three of the girls were close to her size, and Josephine was smaller and could take something and cut it down to make it fit. But a small, cynical voice in the back of Lily's mind warned her not to get involved.

She stood up. "You're welcome to stay another day or two. I'll see if we can spare a little more food tomorrow. I can't promise it, though. Come on, Agatha. Stop begging."

Lily and Agatha went back to Grace and Favor, and Lily pulled the smaller trunk out of the closet and looked over her old clothes. Most hadn't been worn more than once or twice. And they were so out-of-date she'd be embarrassed to wear them now, even if they still fit. She'd been considerably plumper before 1929, and for all Mrs. Prinney's fine cooking, hadn't put back on much of the weight.

"I'll never wear these again," she told Agatha, who cocked her head alertly, as if she understood. "Why am I so reluctant to let them go? The past is the past."

She sorted through the dresses and put about eight out on the bed to study. Four of them were in shades of red and pink and apricot. She set these aside and removed an assortment of shoes she hoped would fit the girls. Two of her perkiest hats had been made to go with two of the dresses, and she set them aside as well. She put the other dresses back.

She considered talking to Robert or Mrs. Prinney about her plan but decided it was really up to her. She'd made her decision. She smiled wryly to herself at the thought of what her mother might have thought about giving half her once-stylish wardrobe to hoboes. She hoped and believed, if her mother had lived in these dreadful times, she'd have done the same thing.

Chapter 19

Jack spent most of the first couple of days hiding out at Mary Towerton's house with his typewriter. He knew no one would be at her house and nobody would think of looking for him there. He was typing out everything he'd seen, heard, thought, remembered, assumed. Thank God he'd rescued his notes! He pounded the typewriter like a madman all night Wednesday, all day Thursday. Someday there might be a book in it. He couldn't possibly compress the experience he'd had to a few newspaper articles. Few people in Voorburg would want to read about it endlessly.

This was a self-revelation that made him feel he'd finally grown up as a journalist. Knowing how much to put in and what to leave out. The editor of a small hometown paper couldn't force too many thoughts and facts down his readers' throats.

The other reason he hid, aside from being distracted, was to be there if Mary and the children made good time returning home. It might take her three days if she pushed the mule hard, as many as five or six if she didn't. The last stage of her journey had to be up one side or the other of the river. Which bridge would she take if she came up the west side, assuming she was sophisticated enough not to attempt to go through New York City proper?

But if her grandfather had taken them down the east side of the Hudson River, she'd come that way because that was the route she knew.

His motorcyle battery had died while he was gone, and the sidecar had a flat tire. He'd borrow Ralph's motorcycle on Saturday, day four, if she hadn't returned by then, and look up and down Route 9 on both sides to the south of Voorburg.

He finally came back down to earth early Friday morning and realized he'd be late with his copy to the printer if he let the Brewsters vet his article. It was time, anyway, to assert his independence. If they wanted to touch a word, he'd quit the job and take his precious editorials elsewhere.

But he needed to tell them this.

He'd return to Mary's house on Ralph's motorcycle and put the typewriter in the sidecar later in the day. He'd carried the heavy, awkward thing here. He wasn't going to carry it back.

He tidied up the house. Put a vase of wildflowers on the kitchen table, in case Mary and the children got home while he was gone. He added a note asking her to let him know when she returned.

Then he took his first article to the printer, and trudged up the hill to Grace and Favor.

"Oh, Jack! Everybody will be so glad to know you're back!" Mrs. Prinney exclaimed, when she opened the door. "When did you eat last? You look so thin and tired! Come in, come in. Nobody's here but me and Mimi right now. I'll make you up a sandwich. Come back to the kitchen."

Lily had dawdled about returning to the old icehouse. She knew it was right to give the girls the clothes they needed, but parting with them was hard. Her mother had bought one of them as a surprise for her eighteenth birthday. Another was one she'd dearly loved and worn to a party that she'd enjoyed enormously. Besides the memories, she had other things to do before she gave them up. But Friday morning, she packed up the dresses, shoes, and hats in old boxes and some more of Mrs. Prinney's food and put it all in a wheelbarrow to take it to the icehouse.

"I'm glad you're taking them your frocks," Mrs. Prinney said. "Did I tell you the girl with the violin case came to the back door to thank me shortly after you gave them food the first time? She asked if she and the others could help with anything, doing laundry, dusting, or such. Wouldn't Mimi have had a fit! But it was gracious of the girl to express her gratitude so nicely and offer to work."

"I suspect she was well raised and well educated," Lily said. "It's not true of the other three, and I think that's why they defer to her judgment."

As Mrs. Prinney was helping Lily arrange things in the wheelbarrow, Lily said, "I went to Jack's office again yesterday to check the mail. His typewriter is missing. I hope nobody stole it, but I also hope it means he's back and is using it somewhere. Okay, I'm ready to go, I think."

Pushing the wheelbarrow along the nearly abandoned path through the woods was harder than she'd expected, especially as Agatha kept running in circles, barking at the squeaks of the wheel and getting in Lily's way.

Naturally this racket alerted the girls, and they met her halfway to help by carrying some of the boxes.

"What's all this?" Judy asked.

"Mostly dresses," Lily said. "And I've spoken to the theater owner. He thinks it would be good both for him and for you to play your music in front before and after the movies."

Two of the girls screeched with delight and wanted to tear into the boxes there and then. "Ladies," Judy warned, "let's be polite about this, please."

The other three ran back to the icehouse with the boxes while Judy took over pushing the wheelbarrow. "You're a good person, Miss Brewster."

Lily shook her head. "Not as good as you think. I tried them all on one last time yesterday, instead of bringing them to you sooner. None of them still fit me. But it was hard to let them go."

"When we make some money, we'll buy you a new one. To remember us by," Judy said.

Lily smiled. "First buy Cynthia a new trumpet. It'll sound much better with a violin than a harmonica does."

"It certainly would," Judy said, with a hearty laugh.

When they caught up with the others, the girls were fidgeting. "Now may we open the boxes?"

Judy nodded, and they ripped into them, exclaiming their delight as each dress, shoe, and hat appeared. The pretty girl said, "Oh, Judy, you must wear the red one! It would be divine on you. And look, the shoes go with it, and a perfect little hat. Try it on right now. Please!"

"Only if you'll try on the one with the pink ruffles. It's simply *you*!"

"You'll have to take it up at the hem," Lily warned. "I'll come back with a needle, thread, and scissors. I meant to bring them and forgot."

The girls abandoned their boy clothes and tried on the dresses with glee. They pranced awkwardly around in the woods in their high heels and hats, complimenting each other. Even Cynthia unbent enough to hug the coral print dress to herself and laugh with delight.

Lily herself couldn't have been happier with

the result. The two girls who still had their long
hair looked lovely. The ones with the short hair-
cuts got the hats and didn't look bad at all. For
all her selfish dithering, she'd never been so
pleased about anything she'd done before.

"Okay, girls, take them back off. We'll have to
go back to that little creek and bathe before we get
them dirty," Judy said.

"Who's going to look out for the creepy man?"
Cynthia asked.

"We'll take turns," Judy said.

"What creepy man?" Lily asked.

Judy explained. "Just this older guy with a suit
and a hat and a satchel. Last time we were cleaning ourselves up in the creek, we noticed him
watching us. When he realized we'd seen him, he
came out of the woods, strutting as if he were
young and handsome, and was vulgar to us.
Wanted to know which one of us wanted to go
into the woods with him first."

"He talked to us like we was whores," Cynthia
said angrily.

"Prostitutes," Judy said. "Not that it's really a
better word. It just doesn't sound quite as nasty,
Cynthia."

"I don't care. He was a nasty man himself,"
Cynthia countered.

I'll bet it was Donald Anderson, Lily thought. I
hope Roxanne never knows.

"You better start cleaning up soon and practic-
ing your music." She would have liked to invite

them to Grace and Favor to bathe in her bathroom, but she wasn't sure Mr. and Mrs. Prinney would approve of going quite that far to help them. "You're expected to start performing this evening."

Judy took the wheelbarrow back for Lily and waited outside the kitchen door for the scissors and thread.

"You just missed Jack Summer," Mrs. Prinney said, when Judy had gone. "He looked awful. I fed him. He said he had to talk with you and Robert later today."

"I'm so relieved to hear that," Lily said. "Did he say what he needed to talk about?"

"Not to me. But he looked terribly serious."

"He would, after what he probably went through in Washington."

Lily went up to her room to wash her hands and face and take a little rest. She was troubled about what the girls had said about the creepy man watching them bathe. She should have asked them when it was. It might not have been Donald Anderson, though the description they gave—a man in a suit and tie and carrying a satchel—certainly sounded like him.

And there was something else she sensed vaguely she should have asked, but it was hiding at the fringes of her mind.

She turned her thoughts instead to the girl band. She'd have to convince the Prinneys, Mimi, and Robert to go to town tonight and cheer the girls on. Somebody had to be the beginning of a crowd, or a crowd wouldn't form. Maybe invite Chief Walker and even Ralph Summer. And she'd done what Mr. Bradley, the greengrocer, asked her to do. She could call in that chip as well.

Chapter 20

Jack Summer and Robert turned up at Grace and Favor within minutes of each other—just coincidentally about half an hour before dinner. The first floor of the mansion smelled divinely of another of Mrs. Prinney's Dutch meals: a creamy cold leek soup and homemade cheesey crackers for starters, a rich rabbit stew with paper-thin onions adorning the top of the bowl, and an enormous salad with a sweet raspberry dressing.

Jack and Robert had settled in for drinks in the library. A slight breeze scented with something floral was coming in from the little balcony beyond the open French doors, mixing wonderfully with the smells of the food being prepared. "Have you heard about our murder yet?" Robert asked.

"The man in the icehouse? Of course," Jack said, sounding preoccupied.

"No, unfortunately that's a bit on hold. The

whole of the Albany police department is looking
for some gangster who's rumored to be in the
area. Legs Diamond, maybe."

"Legs Diamond was killed last month," Jack said.

"That must be why he came to mind. Maybe it
was Pretty Boy Floyd or another one. Didn't your
cousin Ralph tell you about Donald Anderson?"

"He didn't say a word. Who's Donald Anderson?"

"Oh, you've seen him in town," Robert
stretched his legs out and lighted a Cuban cigar.
"The guy who went around looking for work in a
suit and tie, carrying a satchel."

Jack nodded. "He was murdered?"

Robert leaned forward. "That's a bit blasé. It
doesn't interest you? You're the newspaper editor. He was a longtime local."

"I'll have to get the details for next Thursday's
issue. Monday's is already at the printer."

Robert raised an eyebrow. He hadn't seen a
draft of the columns.

"That's what I came to talk about. We'll wait for
Lily, though."

"You'll wait for me? Why?" Lily said, entering
the library with Agatha and an old hairbrush to
comb out the burrs she'd gotten exploring the
back of the icehouse. "Oh, Robert, put that cigar
out. It's stinking up the room and will make my
hair smell like a tavern."

Jack had had enough. He stood up and said de-
fiantly, "I've sent Monday's text to the printer."

"Oh?" Lily said. "I don't remember seeing it."

"And you won't. I've submitted it to you and Robert for almost a year now. It's time to let me do my job without interference. That's why you hire an editor. To use his own judgment."

"We've never questioned your judgment, I might remind you," Lily said, putting down the brush and glaring at him.

"Any time you do, you can fire me. I know that, and you do too. So let's stop making me wait for your opinions."

Robert and Lily exchanged a glance. Lily said, "Robert, remember that conversation we had the other day, about the Russian nobility? I've already described our situation to four strangers." He was obediently putting out the cigar carefully so he didn't lose a single crumb of it.

Jack looked at both of them as if they'd gone utterly mad. Russian nobility?

"Good for you, Lily," Robert crowed, throwing in a little applause. With a nearly maniacal grin, he went on. "Okay, Jack, here's a dose of the truth, and the whole truth. Lily and I don't own the newspaper. We don't own a damned thing. Not this mansion. Not even the Duesie."

"That's a ridiculous thing to say," Jack said. He'd had a hard week, and his patience was as fragile as a cobweb in a storm.

"It's true," Lily chimed in. "Uncle Horatio's will gave us a place to stay, nothing else. Actually, we have to live here for ten years to inherit anything.

Mr. Prinney controls the estate. We've been living a lie for a year, and we're sick and tired of it."

Jack sat down in the chair heavily. "Why have you kept this secret? You mean I really work for Elgin Prinney?"

"No, you work for Uncle Horatio's estate," Lily said. "But Mr. Prinney is fully responsible for it. So I guess you could look at it that way."

Robert chimed in. "The answer to your other question is that we were embarrassed by being poverty-stricken, like nearly a third of the country is now. It just hit us earlier. We had no idea we'd become the norm instead of the exception."

"You don't expect me to believe this, do you?" Jack asked.

"You have to," Robert said. "It's God's own truth."

Lily put down the brush, which made Agatha think she might escape, until Lily put a heavy hand on her. "Oh, Robert. We forgot to tell Mr. Prinney we were going to spill the beans."

"I don't think he'll care," Robert said. "I have the feeling he wasn't ever happy to be sharing our deception. He understood why, I know. But we dragged him into the act. He's too honorable a man to have liked deceiving the townspeople he's known all his life. So, Jack, you've wasted your breath on us. You'll have to fire up your indignation all over again and present your ultimatum to Mr. Prinney." He made a dramatic twirl with the cold cigar.

"Now that we've sorted that out, I want your help," Lily said. "I want you both to go to the movie house this evening. Jack, it's *The Public Enemy*."

"Why does a movie that's been running since last year in New York City take this long to get to Voorburg?" Jack grumbled. This meeting wasn't going the way he intended.

"It's got James Cagney, you know," Robert said. "You could swan around in your checked jacket looking like him."

"I'll see it tomorrow. I'm still too tired." He'd hoped they'd ask him about the Bonus March, but they seemed to have forgotten where he'd been.

"But you *must* go tonight. Just to stand in front for a little while, if nothing else. You'll be surprised by the entertainment," Lily said.

"What's this about?" Robert asked.

"You'll see," Lily said smugly. "It's a little project I took on. Now, Jack, tell us about the Bonus March. You look as if you had a very bad experience."

"Not as bad as the others," Jack said, glad Lily hadn't actually forgotten. "But I'd rather you just read my reports in the paper. I've divided them into four sections. One for each Monday and Thursday, this coming week and the next."

"Can't you even give us a hint?" Robert asked. "We heard and read so many conflicting views and information."

"I'd rather let you read my columns first, if you don't mind."

Agatha yelped slightly as Lily pulled a burr out of the hair near her ear.

"What are you doing to that poor dog?" Emmaline Prinney asked as she came in the library and subsided on a chair by the French doors and fanned herself with a wide wooden spatula.

"Just cleaning her up," Lily said. "Did you fix enough to have Jack to dinner?"

Mrs. Prinney said, "You know me. How could you ask? He must eat with us."

"And after dinner, we all have to go to town and stand in front of the movie house," Lily said.

"I don't know how Elgin will feel about that," Mrs. Prinney said, frowning. "He doesn't like gangster films."

"He doesn't have to go inside," Lily said.

"Curiouser and curiouser," Robert said, rubbing his hands together.

Lily shouldn't have worried about encouraging a crowd. It was the first showing of the long-awaited film, and townspeople had lined up early.

"Who are those deliciously pretty girls?" Robert asked.

"They're a girl band," Lily said. "They have permission to play before the movie and at the intermission while the reels are rewound."

Robert studied the girls, who were setting themselves up on the edge of the road in front of the movie house. They were all dressed up in fancy frocks. One of them had a violin case. The cute little curly-blond one had an empty cigar box covered with flowery wallpaper and little bows.

Suddenly he looked at Lily. "Aren't those girls wearing your dresses? Some of them look familiar."

Lily nodded. "And my hats and shoes. The dresses didn't fit anymore, and they needed them more than I do."

"And I presume you set this up with the owner of the movie house as well?"

"Well . . ."

"You are *such* an interfering woman," Robert said, giving her a little hug. "Where did you find the girls?"

"They're hoboes."

"No! They sure clean up good," Robert said with a laugh.

"I've never heard them play, though. We may all be in for a horrible surprise."

Lily assumed Judy's music education had been classical and they'd do some sort of "high-toned" music, and was surprised when their first piece was a rollicking version of "Turkey in the Straw." Judy was using the violin like a country fiddle, grinning and sawing it enthusiastically. The harmonica accompaniment was perfect. All three—violinist, singer, and harmonica player—wiggled, and smiled, and tapped their high-heeled feet in time to the music.

The smallest hobo girl, Josephine, wearing Lily's ruffled pink dress, was tottering through the crowd as if she were simply listening, but making sure everyone could see the open cigar box in her dainty little hands. A young couple started dancing in line while a few others dropped coins in the cigar box.

Lily liked the clink of money in the box more than she liked the music. She couldn't have been prouder of herself if she'd invented a submarine or a new vaccine. It was the best thing she'd ever done for anyone else, much less strangers. After all her agonizing over giving away the party frocks, she'd done the right thing, and it felt very good to see the result.

Jack smiled, and grabbed Lily for a quick whirl. Even Mr. Prinney was tapping his foot to the music.

Lily laughed out loud.

Robert asked, "What's so funny?"

She leaned up close to him and whispered, "I'm afraid I'm turning into Edith White. I suddenly understand her. I grasp the concept of making other people do what's good for them."

"I thought you always knew. After all," Robert said, "you made us both come to live in Voorburg."

Chapter 21

Saturday morning, Jack rousted Ralph early. "You're not using the motorcycle for anything important today, are you?"

Ralph looked at the clock on the nightstand. "Holy Jesus, Jack. Are you crazy? This is the only morning I get to sleep late."

"Go back to sleep, then. I'll have the motorcycle back by dark and full of gas."

He wasn't sure that Ralph had fully realized what he'd said. If Jack was lucky, Ralph wouldn't go looking for the cycle later and think it was stolen.

Jack had given this trip a lot of thought. He'd decided to take the eastern route down Highway 9 to see if he could find Mary and the children along the way. He hoped she hadn't come that way, through New York City, but she might have been afraid of crossing the Hudson on yet another bridge in a wagon with automobiles zipping along around her.

As he was going south, he saw a number of people going north who looked as if they'd come from Washington: dejected people, looking sick at heart, not families out for a pleasure ride in the country. He thought one group of men walking along the side of the road was slightly familiar. If they were from the area, he might have seen them at the Anacostia Flats.

He slowed the motorcycle and hailed them. "Have you passed a woman driving a mule and cart? She has a boy about three or four years old and a babe in arms. Long blond braid under a red kerchief?"

They didn't even reply except to shake their heads negatively and keep trudging along. They didn't want to meet his gaze.

Jack continued along the road. A cart and mule could have gone faster than men on foot. But he doubted that Mary had gone that fast. She had the children to feed and care for. That would have slowed her down. She probably wouldn't start until daylight and would stop before it got dark.

He was entering Yonkers when he thought he might have spotted her. At least it was a small figure with a mule in front. He gunned the cycle and hurried forward. The woman approaching half stood, shaded her eyes, and started waving. "Mr. Summer, Mr. Summer!" she called out with relief.

The mule didn't like the noise and smell of the motorcycle and tried to go past Jack much too fast. Jack turned the machine off and ran to catch up with them. He leaped into the cart, said hello to the little boy, and climbed in front to take the reins. The mule slowed to a stop.

"I'm so glad to see you," Mary said. "What on earth are you doing here? How far are we from home?"

"Close enough. You'll make it by sundown if you move along."

"But where are *you* going?"

Jack said, as if it were obvious, "I was looking for you. I'll go along in front of you and lead you home. Would your boy like to ride in the side-car?"

Mary grinned. "I think he'd faint away with the thrill if you ask him. It's so fine of you to remember us and help out again. It was such a harrowing, endless drive I honestly wondered if we shouldn't just start our lives over somewhere along the way."

"I'm glad you didn't. I was awfully worried about you—and the children."

Mary glanced at the cot in the back. "The baby slept most of the way. She'll probably be awake for days when we get to Voorburg. I thank you most heartily for coming to look for us. It's so good to see a familiar face." She patted his hand briefly, then looked appalled that she'd done so.

Jack carried the boy back to the motorcycle,

made a wide slow circle around the mule, and slowly started north. The little boy's eyes were as big as melons. At first he clutched the front of the sidecar. Eventually he relaxed and started looking around and giggling. Jack wished there were a way to put the cycle in the wagon and ride with Mary, but it would have taken too much time to lever it up onto the bed of the wagon, even if there had been room for it. He wanted to hear all about her trip. Where had she stayed? What had they eaten? Had the money he'd given her lasted long enough?

But there would be time for all that later, when the family was home safe.

The all-girl band was so successful that they managed to buy Cynthia a third-hand trumpet. Lily was glad to hear it. But after the initial thrill of having helped them started to fade, she got back to wondering about Donald Anderson.

Did Roxanne suspect him of pursuing other women? Maybe not. Roxanne might have been too busy raising the children and growing her vegetables. She probably didn't even have the leisure to wonder where her husband was and what he was really doing most of the time.

Unfortunately, Lily knew that was feeble reasoning. Roxanne wasn't dim. Mightn't it be more likely that she knew and didn't care, for some unimaginable reason?

Lily admitted to herself that she was much younger, and probably still naive about some things. She found it impossible to read an older woman's mind. Especially an older woman with a wandering husband and a houseful of growing children she was lovingly responsible for raising. Obviously most marriages weren't perfect. When she was young, Lily had overheard her mother's friends talk about how irritating they found some of their husbands' traits.

"He just comes home every night and listens to the radio until he falls asleep in his chair," one had said.

"He never wants to go out to dinner and is a picky eater. I'm so sick of hiring one cook after another," another complained.

"I can't sleep for his horrendous snoring. I'm always tired," another woman said, not knowing a child was eavesdropping on her elders.

But these weren't the same things as Roxanne's problem husband. His actions weren't annoyances. They were outright betrayals of their marriage vows. And he'd barely tried to conceal them. Lily thought Roxanne must have known or at least suspected what sort of disloyal man she was married to. If Chief Walker thought so too, Roxanne was going to be in big trouble.

But for all that, Lily simply couldn't imagine such a forthright woman simply bumping off her husband. She didn't *want* to imagine it. Lily had been half joking about turning into an Edith White. She was more interested in being the same sort of woman Roxanne appeared to be: hardworking, sensible, intelligent. Taking good care of her own children and her brother and his motherless daughter.

There were probably quite a number of people who had been glad to be rid of Donald Anderson. Some of the women who'd been victims of his unwelcome advances. Husbands or brothers of those women who cooperated with him or complained about him. Perhaps even people he'd worked for or with. Or just drinking pals he'd offended. The possibilities were endless.

On Sunday, Lily ran into Chief Walker on her way to church. She took him aside to say, "I need to talk to you privately. Would you have a few minutes later?" So after church he was waiting down the block.

The beat-up old black Ford the city provided and maintained for him had peeling white lettering saying CHIEF OF POLICE on the door. She slipped into the vehicle.

"I'd love a ride home. Mr. Prinney went straight off after church to take his wife to visit one of their daughters for the day, and Robert didn't feel like going to church at all."

"Is this what you wanted to talk about?" Walker said with a smile.

"Not exactly, but part of it," she said, smiling as well. "It's about Donald Anderson. I don't know how much you know about him—"

"And I'm not sharing what I do know," he said bluntly. "But feel free to tell me what you think."

As they rode up the long winding road, she explained. "I've spoken to several women in town who told me he'd made unpleasant and unwelcome overtures to them. Sexual, I mean," she said bluntly, trying not to blush at saying the word out loud to a man—and a good-looking young man as well. "I can't tell you who they were; they told me in confidence. One was a woman with a baby he kept asking to hold, and he would touch her in the wrong way when he took the child. Do you know what I mean?"

"I get the picture," Walker said, frowning.

"Another was a single woman who wouldn't even tell me what he said to her, it was so awful and personal."

She looked at him for confirmation. He seemed unaware of her gaze.

"Anything else?" was all he said.

"Just that the last time I saw him, I *think* it was Saturday morning before he died, he had the satchel with him. I heard it was missing when he was found."

"Several people have told me he had it," Howard Walker admitted. "But it's been found and is being examined in Albany."

"Where was it found?" Lily asked.

"That's not information I'm free to give out," Walker said.

Lily wasn't much liking this one-way conversation. She respected his honorable attitude, but it thwarted her curiosity.

When they pulled up in the drive to Grace and Favor Cottage, Lily said, "Dinner is just Robert and me and Mimi. Potluck leftovers. You're welcome to join us."

"Why not? I'm not going to hear anything from Albany on a Sunday." He leaned across Lily and pushed open her door. "I'd enjoy talking to you and Robert and getting to sit down and eat something somebody else cooked."

It quickly became obvious that Walker wasn't going to talk about the murder in front of Lily and Mimi. He and Robert droned on endlessly about the baseball season, comparing pitchers and first basemen. Since neither of them seemed particularly knowledgeable, it was clear they were merely making conversation that would drive the women away from the table as soon as possible.

When Walker left, Lily cornered Robert in the yellow parlor where he'd stretched out on a sofa near the window with the Sunday papers.

"Why won't Howard Walker tell me anything?" Lily asked. "I suspect he's told you everything he knows."

"I think he didn't want to speak about it in front of Mimi."

Lily shook her head. "It wasn't Mimi. It was me. I rode up the hill with him telling him what *I* knew, and he said flat out he wouldn't say what *he* knew."

Robert thrashed a paper into a vertical fold and said, "Maybe it's sex. He might think you don't know about unfaithful husbands."

"I was telling him about the same thing."

Robert finally laid aside the paper and sat up. "This is just a guess. Walker hasn't said this to me, mind you, but I think he greatly admires Mrs. Anderson. Who wouldn't? But murder is most often done by a family member when emotions are running high. I'd feel that way if I were he. Torn between common sense, his own decency, and the unpleasant facts of his job."

Lily nodded in partial agreement. It was a possibility.

"Where did he find the satchel?"

Robert said, "Under Mrs. Anderson's bed."

Lily gasped, "Oh, no! I wouldn't have his job for anything in the world."

Chapter 22

Jack Summer had led the mule up the drive to Mary's house and watered and fed the exhausted animal while Mary put the children down for naps and took her belongings out of the cart.

"I stayed at your house for a couple of days," Jack said, when the mule had been tended to.

Mary Towerton turned around and stared at him. *"What?"*

"I wanted to hide from everyone to get my notes in order so no one could ask me questions. And I also wanted to be here if you got home on your own."

Mary wasn't pleased. "Did any of the neighbors see you?"

Jack was surprised at the question. "I don't know. Look, Mrs. Towerton, I didn't snoop in your things. I didn't mess anything up. I didn't think you'd mind."

"Mr. Summer, I'm grateful for all you've done, but I'm a married woman!"

Jack had been trying hard to forget this. "I know. But you weren't here. I wasn't disgracing you. I was just . . ." His voice trailed off. *Your husband's abandoned you and your children and is never coming back* was on the tip of his tongue.

But he'd never say that out loud. And neither would she.

"I'm sorry," was all he had said. "Someday I hope you'll find the time to tell me about your trip home. I'll be on my way."

"Mr. Summer—"

"No, everything's all right. You're home safe. I'll be getting on now."

He had gone off on Ralph's motorcycle in a few seconds before this unhappy conversation could drag itself out any longer. He felt guilty, of course. He really hadn't had the right to move into her house. He knew that, even though his intentions were good. Or were they? They'd shared an extraordinarily awful experience and come through it. He assumed this made them at least friends. But she *was* a married woman. He'd known that all along.

He went back to the boardinghouse. His cousin Ralph was lounging around on the porch in his undershirt and crummy old trousers.

"You look a mess!" Jack had said irritably. "Why aren't you working on the house we're supposed to be moving into?"

"Why aren't you?" Ralph had thrown back. "And why'd you take my motorcycle?"

"None of your damned business."

Lily decided on Monday that she really needed her hair done by someone who knew how to cut it well. She'd been hacking at it herself for the last few years with her manicure scissors. Besides, hairdressers knew everything about everyone. Nina Pratt, the woman from the Voorburg Ladies League, could tell her a lot about the other women in the group. And she would be an excellent prospect for passing along the knowledge that the Brewster brother and sister weren't the rich heirs that everyone supposed them to be. Now that she and Robert had decided to tell the truth about their situation, they were gleefully spreading the news far and wide.

She asked Robert to drive her to town and hit him with another thing that had been on her mind. "You need to teach me how to drive this monster. I can't keep on asking you to be my chauffeur."

Robert, as expected, was seriously alarmed by this. "I don't mind a bit, hauling you around."

"But I know sometimes it isn't convenient for you."

"Well, maybe someday. But I'll keep the keys, if you don't mind."

Someday, she thought. It better be pretty soon. As much as she loved living in the mansion, there were times she simply wanted to get away and go for a drive and see something new all by herself.

He left her at the hairdresser and said he'd be back in an hour.

"Make it an hour and a half. I need a lot done."

She knocked at the door of the well-kept little house, and a young woman she assumed was Nina Pratt's daughter Helga came to the door. Lily introduced herself and said, "I'm sorry I don't have an appointment. But I'm at my wits' end about my hair. I can wait until it's convenient for your mother to get to me."

"She's free right now," the girl said.

Nina Pratt was glad to see Lily—at first. "I wondered when you'd get around to coming here," she said. "You really need help."

"I really can't afford this," Lily simpered. "You know, I presume, that we really don't own Uncle Horatio's mansion or his other assets."

Nina's smile faded. "No, I didn't know. How is that?"

"Well, he left it to us on the condition that we stay there for ten years and prove to Mr. Prinney that we deserve to have it. Otherwise everything he owned goes to various charities."

Nina's eyes almost sparkled at the news. Lily knew that all the next customers would be told. Hairdressers, in her experience when her family was wealthy, were better and faster than the telegraph at spreading news.

"Anyway," Lily added brightly, "I have a little

money saved up and, as you say, I need help. But I won't be able to afford it very often."

Nina seated her in a chair in front of a mirror on the enclosed back porch, which had been set up as a beauty shop, and ran a comb through her hair, frowning. "You need a good cut. Not a lot shorter, mind, just tidier. You've been doing this yourself, I suppose."

"I'm afraid I have. I wouldn't mind it a bit shorter, but it doesn't have much curl. I think I need a permanent wave as well."

This cheered Nina a bit. "An excellent idea."

While Nina was meticulously going through Lily's hair, snipping off individual sections in tiny bits, Lily said, "I'm so glad I was invited to join the Voorburg Ladies League. Such nice women. But I feel like a stranger there, unfortunately. I don't know much about any of them."

At this Nina smiled. "The things I could tell you!" she said conspiratorially.

"Do. Start with Mrs. White."

"Isn't she a marvel?" Nina said. "Such a good woman, but the bossiest in the world. You know those plates they raffle off at the movie theater every Friday night? She's the one who provides them. She thinks nobody knows it, but everyone does. She keeps her light under a basket."

"Has she lived in Voorburg a long time?"

Nina thought about it for a bit. "*She* has. But I think her first husband and the girl came here around 1922. They'd lived in one of those cold states north of here before. Vermont, maybe."

"What girl is that?"

"A relative of her husband. I think his sister's child. The parents had died in a traffic accident, and Bernard—her first husband—felt they should take her in to raise. Oh, the battles! Edith never had a child of her own and was delighted to have a daughter to mold."

"Then why were there battles?"

"The girl—I think her name was Isabel or Elizabeth—was already about fifteen or sixteen and didn't want to be what Edith wanted." She lifted a chunk of Lily's ragged bangs and peered at them. "Edith wanted to make her into one of those debutantes. She was always nagging her husband to get them an apartment in New York or Chicago where she could introduce the girl to society. Neither her husband nor the girl liked the idea."

"Is she still around? The girl, I mean."

"No, when Edith's husband died so tragically, the girl was of age and bolted. It was ungrateful of her. Edith meant well. She could have arranged a good marriage for the girl to a rich man. The girl was pretty enough to be a debutante and had lovely manners and a sense of style. Edith was crushed when she ran off."

"What a shame," Lily said. "I'd like the bangs to grow out. Don't cut them short, if you don't mind. What do you mean about Edith's first husband dying tragically?"

Nina set about working on the back of Lily's hair. "It's a little wavy back here. We won't need much more curl. The husband died in some sort of water accident way out west. If I'm remembering right, a train he was on went into some big river that was flooding. Almost all the bodies were washed away or trapped in the train underwater. There wasn't a funeral, just a private memorial service at Edith's home. And the moment it was over the girl called a taxi and had him carry her away with trunks full of the lovely clothes Edith had bought her."

"How awful for Edith."

"Nobody ever heard from her again. Edith was slim and pretty then and married Henry White quite soon after. I think she still hoped to have a child of her own to raise. But there never was one."

Lily found herself wondering if Phoebe knew all this. Phoebe pretty much refused to gossip.

"What's Mrs. Rismiller like? She was so quiet at the two meetings I've been to. She seems like a nice woman, but she always looks so tired."

"It's not easy being a minister's wife. And she didn't intend to be one," Nina said. "They married young, when Mr. Rismiller was in college studying to be a doctor, and suddenly he changed his mind after the marriage and wanted to be a minister. Poor Peggy had no choice in the matter. I don't think she quite believes what happened to her life."

"Do they have children?" Lily asked.

"Only one son, and he's gone off the rails. He was going to follow in his father's footsteps but got tangled up in some weird religion that his parents don't approve of. Fortunately he doesn't visit them often, but when he does he always tries to convert them to his views, which Mrs. Rismiller says are too bizarre to even grasp. Now let's get the rollers in and you'll sit over there where the electric machine is. It won't take long. Your hair has a bit of curl to start with. I'll put a fan on you to keep you cool as soon as I get you hooked up to the electricity. I do a very good marcelling, you know."

"What do you mean by hooking up to the electricity?" Lily said with alarm.

"Oh, it's a very low current, they tell me. It just warms up the metal curlers a bit."

"I'm not sure about this. I think I'd rather just pull my hair back and do the curls in rags like usual."

Nina was disappointed, but she said, "Well, maybe next time you come in you'll want to try it."

Highly unlikely, Lily thought. That thing looks like the electric chair at Sing Sing. Then she laughed at herself. She'd never seen the electric chair, but this horrible machine of Nina's *must* look like it.

"I feel so sorry for Mrs. Anderson, losing her husband," Lily said, as Nina started brushing out her hair and using a hot crimping iron.

"I do too. But I think she's better off without him. He was a horrible man."

"Was he?"

"Just a year ago I heard him trying to seduce my daughter, Helga. Asking her if she'd like to go for a walk in the woods with him. Poor girl didn't even know what he was up to. I gave him a piece of my mind, and he's never come around again."

"Did you tell Roxanne about it?"

"Heavens, no! I didn't want to embarrass her."

Lily went outside when Nina had finished with her, feeling that she'd spread some valuable gossip and received a lot in return. But it wasn't relevant to anything she'd been puzzling over.

Come to think about it, why had she asked about the ladies in the Voorburg Ladies League in the first place? She was trying to find suspects for Donald Anderson's murder that would get Roxanne off the hook. It wasn't remotely likely that any of those women had anything whatsoever to do with his death. Why would they?

She brooded over this for quite a while. Maybe the urge to find out more about them was instinctive in some way. After all, they were the only friends Roxanne carved time out in her life for. They were probably as fond of her as Lily was. Maybe one of them had known Donald Anderson far better than she wanted to and wanted to save Roxanne from him.

But certainly not Edith White or the minister's

wife. Apparently Donald only went after younger women.

Or maybe not. And both women had a strong sense of duty to others.

"Hey, Toots! You look like the cat's pajamas," Robert called out from the car as he pulled up in front of the Pratt house. "If you were a platinum blonde and twice as heavy you'd look just like Mae West."

"I'm not sure if that's a compliment or not," Lily said, as she got in the Duesie.

"I picked up a couple of copies of the newspaper Jack wouldn't show us before it went to print. Take a look while I'm driving and tell me what you think."

Chapter 23

Lily read all the way home. When Robert opened the door of the Duesie for her, she'd just finished Jack's long editorial.

"It's titled 'The Ones Who Were There' and says the second in the series will be called 'The Ones Who Were Lost.' "

"But is it good?" Robert asked.

"It's stunning. You must read it for yourself. Did you get another copy for the Prinneys? I think Mr. Prinney will agree that it's time to stop riding herd on Jack."

She took a copy to Mrs. Prinney and left Robert to sit in the car to read his own paper. She sat down in the library with the third copy to read it again more carefully.

Jack had a real gift for making the reader feel as if he or she had been along with him on this extraordinary trip. She could smell the refuse. She pitied those who were giving up and looked

ashamed of themselves. She wanted to brush the
flies and mosquitoes away when he described the
mess tent. She'd just finished the second reading
and was more impressed than before when
Robert burst into the library.

"I've got to call Jack! I've got to know what he
means by saying the second one is 'The Ones
Who Were Lost.' "

"Why?"

"It might give me a clue to the mummy, if it
means what I think."

"Oh. The veterans from Voorburg who didn't
go to the Bonus March?"

"Or weren't there because they were dead,"
Robert said.

Lily shook her head. "My guess would be that
he means the ones who died in the war."

Mrs. Prinney heard this conversation as she entered the library with tears in her eyes. "I never
thought the boy had it in him. I've never read
anything so touching and terrible. Robert, would
you go to town to speak to Mr. Summer instead of
telephoning and be sure my husband's read this
before you go? I think Elgin will be as surprised
and pleased as I am.

"Oh, and, Robert," she went on. "Mr. Bradley is
holding two pounds of asparagus for me. Would
you mind picking it up? Elgin wouldn't remember if I stuck a note about it to his hand. He gets
so busy at his office he almost forgets he has a
home to go to sometimes."

"That's a good idea. Want to come along, Lily?"

"I do. I gush better than you do."

They did as Mrs. Prinney asked and interrupted Mr. Prinney as he was dictating a first draft of a will to his secretary, an elderly woman who looked as if her hair were in pin curls without the pins. "I'll get to it when we're finished with this," he said.

"I think it's best to read it now," Lily said. "Your wife said you should before we talk to Jack."

Mr. Prinney said, "Very well. Wait outside. I don't want you hanging over my shoulder."

He didn't really want to read the article. He'd been too old to go into the army and he'd been responsible for supporting his wife and growing family as well as his parents and a younger spinster sister at the time of the Great War. But he'd always felt guilty about not signing up. And he felt even worse when he lost a younger brother in Belgium, and three clients, who were also his friends, in France.

He came out on the porch when he'd finished and said, "The boy did a damned fine job."

Lily had to force herself not to gasp. She'd never heard Mr. Prinney say such a strong word. "May we tell him so?" she asked.

"Please do. I'll stop by his office shortly and have a talk with him about doing the paper on his own from now on. I didn't think it was wise until a moment ago."

He hailed them as they started toward the Duesie.

"Wait. I've been meaning to tell you two I'm glad you're telling townspeople your situation. Honesty is always the best policy."

Lily was tempted to give the elderly gentleman a hug, but she was sure he'd be embarrassed if she did. Instead, she went back and shook his hand in quite a formal manner and said, "Robert and I agree. And we're glad you're pleased."

Jack already had two people in his office thanking him for publishing the article, an old farmer and his grandson. The old man had a beat-up straw hat in his hand and mud on his shoes. "You're a good fella," he said. "I couldn't go because we had a crop to get in and take care of until harvest, but I'm saving this here article and making my grandson read it every year or two so he'll know what happened."

Robert and Lily waited politely while the farmer wrung Jack's hand, waved his hat to them in acknowledgment of their presence, and took his grandson home.

"He's right, you know, Jack," Lily said. "This is outstanding. I'm glad now you didn't show it to us earlier. I'd have been walking around town all weekend reading it aloud to anyone I could find to listen."

Jack, understandably, looked very pleased and hardly knew how to reply. But he didn't have to because Robert had underlined in red pencil the phrases he'd liked best and read them back to the author.

"Has Mr. Prinney seen it yet?" Jack asked, when Robert ran out of compliments.

"He has. And he's as impressed as we are," Lily reported. "He's finishing up someone's will and said he'd be over to see you in a little while."

Robert pointed to the end of the piece. "What does this mean, 'The Ones Who Were Lost'? The Voorburg men who were killed in the war or something else?"

"The names of the Voorburg men who died in the war will follow the fourth section in a separate box. The second part is about three men who died or disappeared after the war. But it's only a small element of the piece."

Robert rubbed his hands. "Good. I'm not asking to read the article until it's on the stands, but would you tell me their names?"

"Why?"

"Because one of them might be my mummy."

Jack slapped his head. "I forgot to put that in this issue. You should have reminded me!"

"But I couldn't," Robert said. "You were temporarily among the lost yourself."

Jack grinned. "Okay, let me consult my notes."

Lily interrupted. "I've got to pick up asparagus for Mrs. Prinney. You two go over this and I'll be back soon."

They didn't act as if they'd heard her.

Jack said, "One was Butch O'Dwyer. I don't

know his rank. He died on the second anniversary of the end of the war. Drank himself to death and dropped dead in Mabel's. He's not your man. The second was a former mayor, the town doctor, Major Oggleton. He went to the train station with a trunk and a suitcase, and took the southbound early one morning, and was never heard from again."

"When?" Robert asked.

Jack shrugged. "I have no date. You'll have to ask the man who told me when he gets back home. He's camped out in Central Park, as far as I know."

"Who was the third?"

"A Captain VanZillen. A businessman who died in an accident of some sort out west. Drowned."

"So the one I need to find out about is this Oggleton chap," Robert said, jotting down the name in a little pocket notebook.

"I suppose so," Jack said. "Could you let me know what you find out? I can still slip something about him into the Thursday issue."

"Did this Oggleton leave a family behind? Could they tell me when he left?"

"I don't know. You'll have to run down some old-timers who were his patients. Maybe one of them will remember."

"Would there have been a mention of it in the local newspaper back then?" Robert asked. "That is, if I can pin down an approximate time."

"The few old newspapers that still exist are kept in the basement of the town library," Jack said.

"I didn't know there *was* a basement. I'll work on this," Robert said, rising from the window where he was perched. "Jack, again, you did a terrific job, and I can hardly wait for what comes next."

As Robert and Lily drove home, Robert said, "He only had three men who had died that he knew of. One, a guy named VanZillen, was in an accident out west, Butch O'Dwyer died at Mabel's, and one simply disappeared. Got on a southbound train with his things and rode away. But he was the town doctor and once the mayor of Voorburg, so Jack says some residents are bound to remember him and maybe even know when he left. If it was after 1925, I'll go see if there was anything in the newspaper archives at the library. This guy's name was Major Oggleton, Jack says. That's all he knows about him. Ever heard of him?"

Lily said, "Afraid not. Find your old-timers first. Find a couple of them, if you can. Then I'll help you hunt through the old issues of the papers. Are you sure your mummy was put in the icehouse in 1926?"

"Not exactly. That's what Mimi suggested. Sometime between February and Christmas. But of course, the icehouse was locked by late December. Mimi didn't, and couldn't, have seen a body in there. Someone might have had a key and put him in there later. The pathologist is very reluctant to name even a year of death."

"Why do you care so much about this?" Lily asked. "Whatever family or friends he might have had must have put his disappearance well behind them and gotten on with their lives."

Robert was stymied himself by this question. "Because I found him, I suppose. I'm responsible for finding out who he was."

"But you're not. It was just a coincidence that you were there and were the first to see him. If one of the Harbinger boys had gone in first, would you have expected them to investigate?"

"No, but the Harbinger boys have jobs. And I don't," he said, with genuine sadness.

Lily hated seeing Robert truly unhappy with himself. "Neither do I," she admitted. "But living comfortably in a mansion, eating good food—are we entitled to take someone else's job over?"

"No, Lily. We have to create our own jobs." He thought for a moment and forced himself to sound chirpy for Lily's sake—and his own. "We could call ourselves the Sleuthing Siblings."

Lily laughed. "I think not. And I understand your feelings a bit. They're a lot like mine about the girl hoboes. Nobody asked me to help them. I just needed to do it for my own good."

"I still think we had a good idea with hosting celebrities and making people pay to meet them. It went badly awry the first time, through no fault of our own, but we shouldn't forget it. Great-uncle Horatio's will demands that we earn our living, not just coast along doing good works for free."

"Who's going to pay us for being Sleuthing Siblings?"

"Good question," Robert said grimly.

They arrived home. Robert opened the door of the Duesie for Lily and took her package. "Would you like a stalk of asparagus up your nose?" he said, wishing to cheer her up.

"Not now, maybe later," she said.

Which made him laugh like a loon.

Chapter 24

As Robert was approaching the library the next day, he glanced toward the train station and, on a fortunate whim, altered his course. The stationmaster, Mr. Buchanan, was at his window, reading a book.

"Mr. Buchanan, how long have you had this job?" Robert asked.

"Since Hector was a pup. Started as a baggage handler when I was seventeen. Worked my way up. Why do you ask?"

"I'm trying to find out about a man who lived here named Oggleton."

"Whaddya need to know?"

"When he left town for good."

"That's an easy one," Buchanan said, putting the toothpick he'd been holding in the corner of his mouth into the book as a marker. "I remember because he'd just delivered our youngest boy two days before. The fifteenth of October, 1927. No, I'm getting it wrong: 1926."

"The boy was born that day? Or was it the day Oggleton left?"

"Roddy was born the fifteenth. Dr. Oggleton left the seventeenth."

Robert could hardly believe his luck. He jotted the date in his notebook. "Did he leave any family behind?"

"No. His wife had died of measles a year or so earlier, and they didn't have children."

"And nobody ever heard anything of him again?"

"In a manner of speaking, that's right. But I was on duty and noticed he had his name and address on his trunk and suitcase as well. And about a year later, they were sent back from the city train terminal marked UNCLAIMED PROPERTY."

"What do you think happened to him?"

"I have no idea. Probably leaped off the train at some dangerous spot. He was a really sad man after his wife died."

"Did he say anything to lead you to think that's what he was planning?"

"Didn't say a word. I could be wrong, of course. Maybe he just couldn't stand it here and wanted to make it look like he was taking a trip. And left his things unclaimed because he didn't want any reminder before starting a new life."

"Did you open the trunk and suitcase?"

"Yeah. But not for a month or so. With the new baby in the house, crying all the time, I didn't have the energy. He was the only one of ours with the colic and he cried most of the time for a year and a half. My wife and I nearly went crazy."

"What was in the trunk? Do you remember?"

Buchanan thought for a bit. "His medical bag. I gave that to Dr. Polhemus later. His second best suit. He was always a snappy dresser. Underwear. A lot of medical books. Gave those to Polhemus, too. Oh, and his uniform from the war, the whole thing—boots, socks, puttees, helmet, mess kit, and all. I found a museum that wanted the uniform."

"And the suitcase?"

"Just the usual things. It was a sort of Gladstone bag but smaller than most. A change of shirts and underwear. Another medical book. Toothbrush and powder. Shaving tackle."

Robert had been writing furiously. He put his notebook back in his pocket and thanked Buchanan. "If you think of anything else about him, let me know, would you?"

"Okey-doke. Why are you wondering about him?"

"I'm trying to figure out whose body was found in our icehouse." Robert suddenly realized he had one more question. "Did you see him get on the train?"

"I hoisted his trunk into the baggage car, I remember. It was heavy. But like I say, we had this squalling kid and I was too tired to hang around. I don't remember if he got on the train or not. I just figured he had."

"Could he have just sent his luggage on, then? And walked back through town?"

"I guess it's possible. But why would anyone do that?"

"Good question. Thanks again."

With a specific date in mind, Robert headed straight for the library. He wouldn't need Lily to help. There might have been some sort of notice of his departure. The newspaper was still largely made up of announcements, like "Mrs. Blahblah and her lovely daughter embarked yesterday to visit Mrs. Blahblah's family in Toledo to attend a family party honoring Mrs. Blahblah's father's eightieth birthday."

But his luck turned at the library. The librarian, the young Miss Philomena Exley, was helping a housewife find a specific cookbook. "What newspapers we have are shelved at the north end of the basement. I'm afraid there's no index. I'll help you in a moment."

Robert found the shelves but couldn't determine what was where. The old versions of the *Voorburg-on-Hudson Times* were in order part of the time, but then a batch of earlier or later issues were jumbled in. And many of them had articles cut out or whole pages missing.

Miss Exley came down the steps, and Robert couldn't help but appreciate what lovely legs the young woman had. "I've been working on sorting those out for the last two years," she said. "I haven't made much progress."

"How'd they get in such a mess?"

"The former librarian was an enthusiastic volunteer who knew nothing about how libraries were meant to function, I'm afraid. He let people cut bits out instead of copying them by hand. And just dumped them periodically in any old pile that wasn't already sliding off the shelves. What are you looking for?"

"Any mention of a Dr. Oggleton in 1926."

"That's pretty specific. I'll take a look when I next have a little free time."

"My sister's offered to help me, too."

"Miss Lily? She's on her second round of reading through all our mystery books. She's a lovely girl."

"Sometimes she is," Robert said with a smile. "Sometimes not. I'll see if I can drag her down here to help me tomorrow."

He went to find Howard Walker next. Howard wasn't very interested in Robert's mummy, but Robert wanted to tell him what information he'd discovered.

Howard had news, too. "The guy in Albany has finally gone over the satchel. He says it was empty. Covered, of course, with Ralph Summer's greasy fingerprints and smeared prints from where he held it against his shirt."

"Did someone wipe off even Donald Anderson's prints?"

"No. Ralph just messed up any underlying prints there might have been. But the lining had some tiny shreds of good paper. Probably a résumé of his work that he carried around. Also a lot of vegetative material. Tiny bits of potato skin and some carrot and celery foliage."

"That's not surprising," Robert said. "Mrs. Anderson, I hear from Lily, went on and on about raising the best carrots in town when they were discussing this shopping truck idea. She probably sent vegetables along with him to eat while he was looking for jobs."

"Shopping truck?"

Robert put a hand up. "Don't ask. It's a harebrained idea that Mrs. White is forcing on the Ladies League. You get scrip for what you bring in and can trade the scrip for other stuff. No money changes hands."

"Doesn't sound harebrained to me. It could be a good idea," Howard said. "Maybe I could unload my box of cheap peanut butter."

"Don't let anyone know you like the idea, or you'll put yourself in danger of Mrs. White's coercing you to drive the truck around the countryside. Did the guy in Albany have anything else to say about the satchel?"

"All sorts of things that don't matter. Where and when it was probably made. He thinks it was five years old. Described the leather and hardware it was made of in excruciating detail. Measured every part of it in hundredths of an inch. Useless information."

"May I tell you what I think I've learned about the mummy?"

"Have you really found out anything?"

"Not for sure, but I'm trying to find out more about a Dr. Oggleton. Jack was told at the Bonus March that he wasn't there because he disappeared one day. Just got on a southbound train and was never seen again. Or maybe, according to Mr. Buchanan, *didn't* get on the train at all. He was supposed to be a very snappy dresser. Good suits. And he did his supposed bolt, Mr. Buchanan says, on October seventeenth, 1926."

"Buchanan remembered this exact date? Why?"

"Dr. Oggleton bolted two days after delivering Buchanan's last child."

"What else do you know about this Oggleton?"

"Not much. His wife had died a year or so before. He was deeply saddened by her death. I tried to look through the local newspapers for 1926, but they're a mess. Miss Exley and Lily are going to help me sort them out and see if I can learn anything else about him."

"Let me know if you find out something useful," Howard said. He didn't sound the least bit hopeful that this would happen.

Lily, meanwhile, was walking through a shortcut in the woods to the Anderson house. This was the third time she'd called on Roxanne, but Roxanne was always too busy to sit down for a chat or even to eat much of the food that neighbors were still bringing. Her husband's body had been released for burial the next morning, and Lily was taking her a black straw hat with a dark veil in case she needed it.

As Lily approached the house, she heard a muffled scream and started running. When she got to the house, Roxanne was sitting at the bottom of the rock face that edged her front garden, nursing her knee.

Her brother was frantic. "I'll go to a neighbor and call an ambulance to get you to the hospital!"

"No, you won't. I was more surprised than hurt when I backed off the edge. I'll be okay."

"No, your knee is bleeding," Eugene insisted.

"What's a little blood?" Roxanne stood up and tried out the knee by lifting it up. "Nothing's broken, Eugene, now stop your fretting."

"You could get an infection. You should go to a doctor."

"I'll just wash it off. It'll be okay," Roxanne insisted.

Lily joined them and rolled up Roxanne's dungaree past the knee. The wound was still bleeding, but not in gushes. "Come on inside and I'll wash out your dungarees after I put some peroxide on this," Lily said.

"Shouldn't she use alcohol?" Eugene asked. "Here, let me carry you inside."

"You'll do no such thing, Gene. I'm really all right. Let Lily and me tend to this."

He insisted if she didn't need carrying, she at

least had to lean on his arm. Roxanne glanced at Lily and smiled, half-apologetically. "Just keep an eye on the children, Gene, while Lily fixes me up."

He was reluctant to leave, but finally did so when Roxanne started to unfasten her dungarees. She sat down at the kitchen table, extending a long leg on another chair, wincing as Lily dabbed her knee clean and tied a fresh dish towel around it. Then Lily went upstairs to get Roxanne a skirt to put on.

"What's that in the bag you brought?" Roxanne asked, tugging the skirt over her head.

Lily pulled out the hat. "Phoebe had this in her shop and asked me to drop it off."

"It's a lovely hat." Roxanne stroked the shiny, elaborately woven and highly varnished black straw. "Mrs. Rismiller loaned me a black dress. It's quite long on her, but just long enough on me to cover my knee. I haven't bought a black dress since my mother died so long ago, and that one doesn't fit anymore."

"I think you can always trust a minister's wife to have an extra black dress," Lily said. "Now, you better get outside before your brother thinks you've bled to death."

"Poor Gene. He worries so about me. Thank Phoebe for the loan of the hat. I'm sorry, but I have to get back to work. There are some kind of bugs on the watermelon foliage I've got to get picked off and drowned in a tin can, before the fruits are ruined."

After Lily set the blood-soaked knee of the dungarees in peroxide in a kitchen bowl, she trudged back up the hill, musing that the woman was burying her husband the next morning but was still more concerned about her garden. But then, she couldn't be blamed for insensitivity. The garden provided for her family, no matter what else was happening in Roxanne's hard life.

Chapter 25

It seemed as if half the town came to the funeral. Not for Donald's sake but out of respect for Roxanne. Eugene cried. The children looked confused and frightened. Roxanne stood tall, all in black, mute and expressionless. She only appeared to relax slightly after the cheap coffin was lowered into the ground.

The only notable person in town who didn't attend was Howard Walker. He'd told Robert to observe Roxanne in his stead. He felt the sheriff shouldn't be there and cast a further pall on the event.

"I don't see why not," Robert said.

"Because everyone would be watching to see if I arrested her at the end of the service."

"Are you going to arrest her?"

"I hope not," Walker replied.

Robert was surprised when Eugene, still red-eyed, asked to speak to him privately after the service.

"I want you to thank your sister for getting those hobo girls a job that keeps them away from my sister's vegetables."

"Do you know for sure that's who's stealing them? Have you seen them do it?" Robert asked. "There are a lot of hoboes around these days."

"I haven't exactly seen them do it. But lots of times after dark I go outside with my pellet gun to scare off the raccoons and deer, and I've heard them talking and laughing in the woods. I can't let anyone or anything steal from Roxy. She works too hard to have that happen to her. Thank your sister for me. They haven't been around since she set them up as a band. It was a good thing she did."

"Why couldn't he have told me himself?" Lily asked, when Robert told her what Eugene had said.

"Probably doesn't like to talk to women, except his sister. He's such a quiet, shy fella."

"He's awfully protective of her." She described the incident the day before with Roxanne's skinned knee. "It's good that he's so devoted to her, being as her no-good husband wasn't."

"Are we supposed to be going to the Anderson house now with casseroles and flowers?" Robert asked.

"No, Roxanne said she didn't need any more company or food and just wanted to go home and tend her garden."

"Then how about we go to the library this afternoon? Let's go home and put on the worst clothes we have. It's grim in that basement."

"Good idea. And I've got books to return. Don't let me forget to take them along."

Hours later they were about to give up. They were hot and gritty with dust in their hair and newsprint ink all over their hands. They'd gone through all the 1926 newspapers they could locate and found no mention at all of Dr. Oggleton. Lily was picking through the last mangled paper when she said, "Oh, here's something about a VanZillen. Wasn't that one of your names?"

"What is it?" Robert said, wiping his brow and getting a black streak on his forehead.

"A notice of a memorial service for a Captain VanZillen that had already occurred the week before. It lists his military credits, where he served, and says he died when a ferry crossing the Mississippi capsized during a flood the month before. Nearly sixty people died and were washed away. The service was private," she said, skimming the article. "A Reverend Hale gave the sermon—that must have been before the Rismillers came here. Oh, and the eulogy was by Henry White. That must be Edith's husband. Nothing else of note."

"What was the date?" Robert asked.

Lily flipped the tattered newspaper around. "First week of August. May we go home now?

I'm longing for a shower and clean clothes, and it's almost dinnertime."

"I can't do much more about my mystery mummy until the other vets get back in town. Might as well put him on the back burner for a while. Are you getting more books before we go?"

"I'm much too dirty to touch a book. I'll come back tomorrow."

It wasn't until another three days had passed that Lily had her idea. She thought it was so absurd and unpleasant that she couldn't think of telling anyone and merely said she had some shopping to do in the city and took the 10 A.M. train. One of her suspicions was verified at the New York Public Library. She needed to find out a few more things, and it was going to require getting a permanent wave. If she was right, it would break her heart, but she'd have to tell Howard Walker.

Meanwhile, Robert was also troubled by something that kept nagging at the back of his mind. He couldn't bring himself to mention it to Lily until he knew more. He hunted down the girl band, which wasn't easy, as they'd moved out of Voorburg and gone to Poughkeepsie, where there were more places where they could perform. When he ran them down at last, he had two questions for Judy, their leader.

"My sister told me about the man who was watching you ladies bathe in a creek. She said he talked to you as if you were prostitutes."

"Unfortunately, he did. It was most insulting. Especially when that woman in the tight red dress who hangs out on the street in Voorburg really is one," Judy said.

"I've got another personal question to ask you. I hope you'll answer. It might solve a murder."

Her reply was what he'd feared he'd hear. He went looking for Chief Walker and laid out his theory, which made him sad. He hoped Walker could confirm that he was wrong, but it was out of his hands.

Lily was forced to get her hair done again. She endured the permanent wave curlers and the scary electrical gadget. Afterward, while Nina was trying to get a comb through the result, Lily asked if she knew who Edith White's first husband was. Edith had only referred to him as Bernard in her hearing. Lily got the reply she expected and, with her hair fried to a crisp, reported everything she'd learned to Walker, two hours later.

He stared at her hair, horrified, the whole time she spoke.

When she got home, Mrs. Prinney was equally appalled at Lily's appearance and made her wash her hair twice, put glops of mayonnaise on it, and wrap a steaming hot towel around her head for half an hour. It helped a little.

Two days later, when Howard Walker had done his best to organize and double-check the information he'd gotten from both the Brewsters, he

called Grace and Favor in the morning and asked
for Robert.

"We've got a long day ahead of us. I need you
and Lily to go along with me to make a couple of ar-
rests. I'm taking Harry Harbinger instead of Ralph,
and I'd like you and Lily to meet me at ten o'clock."

Robert parked the Duesie at the bottom of the
Andersons' drive, just out of sight of the house.
Walker arrived a few minutes later, and they
squeezed into his small car for the rest of the drive.

"I want you to get the children outside and ask
them to show you what they do in the garden,"
Walker told Lily. "Do you have a good supply of
riddles to keep them busy?"

"I can think of a few," Lily said.

As it was, the whole family was outside weeding and watering when they arrived. Lily duti-
fully cornered the children while Howard asked
Eugene, Roxanne, Harry, and Robert to come in
the house.

"What's this about?" Roxanne said. "We're
very busy."

"It's about your husband's death, Mrs. Anderson. Please come inside quietly."

They all perched on chairs around the big table
in the kitchen. Walker said, "Robert, tell everyone
what the girl hobo with the violin told you."

Robert, looking extremely uncomfortable, said,
"Lily told me that they'd said a man meeting Mr.
Anderson's description had propositioned them.
I went to the leader of the group and asked this

question—what did he offer you for your 'services'? The leader told me he'd offered them fresh vegetables. Showed them a satchel full of baby carrots, red lettuces, and white radishes before they told him to get lost."

Roxanne's eyes were wide open, her face a mask of anger. "My vegetables," she said, through clenched teeth.

"Robert, tell Mrs. Anderson what her brother said to you."

It was agony for Robert, but he spoke up. "Eugene said that *nobody* could get away with stealing from his sister. He was speaking of the girl hoboes."

"But I believe he was speaking of someone else as well," Howard said. He looked at Eugene, who was busy fidgeting with the salt shaker on the kitchen table and wouldn't meet anyone's eyes.

"Eugene?" Roxanne said softly, putting her hand over his.

After a moment of silence, Eugene leaped from the chair and headed for the back door.

Roxanne, her voice pitched low, in the tone of the mother of mothers, said, "Eugene. Don't you dare open that door. Sit back down."

He turned and stumbled back to the table and slumped in his chair. Grabbing his sister's hands, he said, "I killed him, Roxy. I didn't mean to, but I did it."

Walker said gently, "Tell us what happened, Eugene."

In a shaking voice, still staring at his sister, he told what he'd done. "I was sitting out there in the dark late that Saturday night with my pellet gun, waiting to catch the girl hoboes stealing the vegetables. I meant to sneak up on them and fire the pellet gun in the air to scare them into never coming here again."

"And who did you see?" Harry Harbinger asked. "We're your friends. You can tell us."

"Donald. He was picking Roxy's vegetables."

Roxanne bowed her head in despair.

"I was so angry," Eugene went on, a little more calmly. "I put down the pellet gun and went around the other side of the house, where I thought he'd go. I followed him clear down to town. There was only moonlight and it was hard to keep track of him in the darkness, what with him in his dark suit and hat. When he hurried along the railroad tracks, I stayed well back."

"Where did he go?" Walker asked.

"To the little shed where that woman in the red dress who hangs around town, smoking and flirting, takes her customers. It's hidden in the woods up above the tracks. I'd seen her take a man in there months ago, when I was looking through the woods for mushrooms for Roxy to sell. I know all about which are good ones and bad ones."

"You do, Gene," Roxanne said, with a slight smile.

"I waited about half an hour, and when he came back out with the satchel, I called to him. I was gonna say that if he ever did this again I'd tell Roxy about his stealing and whoring."

"What did he say?" Harry asked, in his kindly, soothing voice.

"I never got to speak to him. There was one of those old metal-handled oars on the ground and he picked it up and ran after me, swinging it at my head. I'm not very fast anymore, ever since I broke my ankle two years back, so I dodged and got behind him and knocked him to the ground and took away the oar. I'm slow, but I'm stronger than he was. I held the oar tight, and then I saw a flash of light as he pulled something out of the satchel that he still had with him. It was a knife, I guess for that woman to cut up the vegetables. Roxy's kitchen knife. He'd stolen that as well."

Roxanne put her hands over her mouth for a moment. "I thought one of the kids had taken it to dig in the dirt, and I didn't believe them when they claimed they hadn't."

"He came at me with the knife. I'd used it lots of times. I knew how sharp Roxy kept it. I knew he'd catch up with me if I ran away. So I swung the metal end of the oar at him."

From outside, they could hear the children laughing at something Lily must have said to them.

"I didn't mean to kill him, just stun him enough to get the knife away from him." Tears came to his eyes. "Swear to God, Roxy, I didn't mean to kill him."

With a half sob in her voice, she said, "I know, Gene. You wouldn't kill anything on purpose." She looked questioningly at Walker.

"He can plead self-defense," Walker said. "But I need to know the rest, and so will the judge."

Eugene haltingly explained that he'd moved the body so it wasn't lying there in the open. He considered going straight to Chief Walker and telling him but was afraid he wouldn't be believed. So he threw the oar and the knife way out into the river on the other side of the tracks where the water was deep and they'd sink right down. But he was afraid the satchel would float, so he took it with him.

"Why on earth did you do that?" Robert asked.

"I dunno. I couldn't think of how to get rid of it," Eugene said. "I put it under my bed. Then in the morning, while Roxy was out in the garden, I moved it under her bed."

"Why?" Roxanne asked.

Eugene looked around at all of them as if it were obvious and finally said, "I knew that nobody who knew how smart and good Roxy is would even think she could have been stupid enough to hide it there herself. People hereabouts think I'm the stupid one."

Chapter 26

Chief Walker sent Eugene along with Harry Harbinger to the police station in the official car to have his statement taken down. Robert pulled Lily aside and told her what Eugene had said.

"Did you believe him about not meaning to kill Donald?" Lily asked.

"A hundred percent. I don't think Eugene knows how to make up a good story."

"How did you figure out that it was Donald stealing the vegetables?"

"I asked Judy what he'd offered for the girls' services."

Lily put the heel of her hand to her forehead. "I'd thought about asking that and then forgot it. What will happen to Eugene?"

"I can't even guess."

Meanwhile, Roxanne was asking Howard Walker the same question.

"The worst thing that can happen is that he

goes to trial and is convicted," Walker said. "But I don't think that'll happen. He's a simple man in the sense that he has no guile. If he tells the absolute truth as convincingly to an attorney, the judge, and the county prosecutor as he told it to us, he'll most likely be dismissed."

"Then that's what I must hold out for," Roxanne said, with a sigh. "I know he's telling the truth. I've never heard him lie. And I have lots of experience hearing lies and recognizing them," she said wryly. "My husband did nothing but lie for years. Will Gene have to be in jail somewhere until this is worked out?"

Walker realized these were exactly the right questions Mrs. Anderson was asking and wasn't the least surprised. She had a way of spotting the center of a problem and taking it on. "I hope not. I'll tell the prosecutor that he's no danger to anyone."

"I'll have to get a lawyer for him. Would you recommend one?"

"You should ask Mr. Prinney. I don't think he has much experience in criminal matters, but if he doesn't want to take it on, he'll tell you who should."

"Does everybody have to know about this?"

That was the question he'd been fearing she'd ask. "Not if I can help it, but court records are public if people want to look at them. Unless the judge chooses to seal the record. You should ask Mr. Prinney about that as well."

Roxanne rubbed her arm and suddenly looked up at the sky. "Oh, my gosh! I think it's starting to rain at last!"

Robert and Lily had noticed this too and approached Walker and Roxanne. "We better get a move on," Robert said. "Mrs. Anderson, I'm sorry I involved myself in this. And I'm sorry for Eugene."

"You've all done your best and you were kind to him," she said, shaking hands quite firmly and formally with Howard Walker. "The truth is better for Eugene and me than yet another lie."

"I'll send Eugene back to you within an hour or two if I can," Walker said.

The Brewsters and Walker got in the Duesie and drove off. "The next job is going to be a lot harder," Howard said.

Walker returned to the jail, checked with Harry on the progress of Eugene's confession, and, satisfied that it was almost exactly the things he'd said before, went back to the Duesie, where Robert and Lily were waiting.

"All right. Let's finish this up."

A few minutes later, they arrived at Edith and Henry White's home. Walker asked the maid if he and his temporary deputy (indicating Robert, who looked surprised at this description) and Miss Brewster could see Mr. White for a few moments.

Henry White didn't look the least alarmed to see the Chief of Police in his front parlor. "Gentlemen and ma'am, will you sit down? What have you called on me for?"

He took the best chair by the fireplace. Lily and Robert sat together on a delicate pink velvet sofa, and Howard remained standing.

"Have you heard about the body that was found on the Brewsters' property last week?"

"Who hasn't?" Henry said pleasantly. "The town's abuzz about it. I'm frankly surprised that no one found it earlier."

"Then you knew about it all along?" Walker said, astonished at this remark.

"I put it there years ago. Would you excuse me a moment while I fetch my wife? She'll need to hear this from me."

"I'll come with you," Walker said.

"Don't worry, Chief Walker. I'm not leaving the house."

He was still behaving as though this were a purely social call. Walker stood at the bottom of the stairs and waited. A few minutes later, Henry came back, arm in arm with Edith, who was asking questions. "Is this about Mr. Anderson? Neither of us knows anything about it."

"No, my dear. It's about me. And you. And Bernard."

"Bernard?" she said, thoroughly confused.

Henry took her to the parlor and made her sit in the best chair while he stood slightly behind her with his hand on her shoulder. "Tell my wife what you're asking me about."

"It's about the body found in the abandoned icehouse at the Brewsters' place," Walker said, every bit as confused as Edith was for the moment.

Edith glanced up at her husband and then back to Walker. "What can that possibly have to do with us?"

"Quite a lot, my dear," Henry said. "This is going to be hard on you. So buck up, my dear."

"Sir, did I understand you to say that you put that body in the icehouse?" Howard asked.

"I did."

"Would you mind telling us why?" Howard was falling in with the social aspect of this bizarre conversation.

"Because he was dead," Henry said, "and I didn't know where else to put him."

Edith tried to stand and face him, but he kept his hand on her shoulder. "What in the world are you people talking about?" she said, outraged.

Henry sighed. "This is a rather long story and I'll start at the very beginning. Edith doesn't know about this and it will be a shock to her, but I think it's time she learns that I fell deeply in love with her at first sight."

"Oh, Henry—" she began.

"And I've never changed my mind."

Lily and Robert exchanged glances. Robert whispered, "What the hell is going on here?"

Lily shushed him.

"I also admired her husband, Bernard

VanZillen, when we first met," Henry continued. "But not for long. He was a harsh man. Brilliant, an excellent businessman at the top of his own heap, but personally as mean as a wolverine. No, Edith, don't say anything yet. When I first met Mrs. VanZillen, she had a cast on her arm—"

"I broke it when I slipped in the kitchen on some spilt coffee and hit my elbow on the counter," Edith said.

"No, darling, you didn't. That's just what you told people. Bernard broke your arm, didn't he." It wasn't a question.

She turned her face away from all of them, deeply embarrassed, and said nothing.

"And six months later, she had a broken leg. She told everyone she'd been in a taxicab accident in New York City, but that wasn't true either."

Lily realized her jaw had dropped, and closed her mouth. "You mean he beat her?" she blurted out.

"Brutally," Henry said, no longer smiling. "And repeatedly. Every time his sister's daughter was away from home. Never in front of the child, isn't that right, my dear?"

Edith had tears in her eyes and her handkerchief to her nose. She nodded.

"My father beat my mother," Henry said. "I knew the signs. I knew the stories women made up to hide the fact. One night when I heard that Elizabeth had gone to spend a couple of days with a school friend in Cold Spring, I decided to

drop in on the VanZillens. I hadn't even reached
the door before I could hear sobbing. I rushed
into the house. Found them in this very room."
He pointed at the middle of the floor. "He had her
down there, hitting her on the head and shouting
obscenities."

Edith looked surprised at this. Lily wondered
why.

"I tried to pull him off her, but he was completely out of his mind with fury. He would have
killed her in another moment. I picked up that
lamp"—he pointed at a heavy bronze statue with
a lampshade on the top of its head—"and I
bopped him with it."

"Henry, you didn't!" Edith cried.

"I did. You were unconscious by this time, your
face bloody. I scooped you up and drove you to a
private sanatorium where I knew the chief of staff
well. For a pretty penny, I demanded the best
treatment and secret medical files. I will be happy
to sign an order releasing them to you, Chief
Walker. You'll see how badly injured she was."

"I'd appreciate it if you would do that," Walker
said. "Go on."

"I sat with Edith until they assured me she
wasn't going to die of her injuries. Then I went
back to their house to tell Henry I was reporting
him to the police and intended to see that he went
to jail. But he was dead. I thought with his rock-
hard head I'd just rendered him unconscious, but
after sitting down in this chair for a while, I de-

cided hiding the body was the only way to save
Edith's good reputation. Wives were blamed
when their husbands beat them, and they still
are."

"Usually," Howard said quietly.

"But I had to get rid of the body. I'd visited old
Horatio one day shortly before and had to go out
in the woods where he had some men clearing
out the icehouse and closing it up. The old boy
said he might find some other need for it someday, maybe tool storage, because there was another ice shed attached to the mansion.
Fortunately for me, he didn't get around to it before he died. So before it got light, I hauled
Bernard's body out to the garage, pulled my car
up, and drove without lights as close as I could
get to the old icehouse. The key was still in the
lock. I threw it away later."

His tone was impersonal, almost as if he were
telling them a story he'd read in a magazine.

Edith was openly crying now, and Lily was
sniffling. Robert was frozen into place.

In a very calm voice, now that the worst of the
story was over, Henry went on. "But there had to
be some way of explaining what had become of
him, and it was up to me to find it. I made up a
story and claimed I'd read it in a Chicago paper,
knowing I was the only one in town who received
that particular newspaper. I invented a ferry accident on the Mississippi River. I knew they happened frequently, as I'd seen such articles in the

past. And most of the bodies got caught in the current and never were recovered."

"And you made up the flood as well," Walker said.

"Oh, the flood. I'd forgotten that part. Yes. I imagine you found the memorial service article. It was an unnecessary detail. I should have left it out."

"Someone else pointed it out to me," Walker said. "And my informant also went through the New York newspapers and found no mention of a flood or a ferry accident."

Robert looked at Lily. Without turning to him, she nodded slightly.

Henry leaned down and kissed Edith on the cheek. "I'm glad I saved your life, dear. I'm glad you never knew it. And I'd do it all over again if I had to, for the years of joy you've given me."

She stood and embraced him.

But he kissed her again and held her out at arm's length, saying, "Chief Walker probably has to put handcuffs on me now, darling."

Chapter 27

Howard was invited to dinner at Grace and Favor that evening. Eugene had been returned home promptly, and Roxanne had come by already to explain to Mr. Prinney about Eugene. Edith White had already tearfully telephoned him as well.

It was understood by all of them, except for Mimi, who'd gone to visit her dreadful aunts that evening, that what was said at the table was confidential. Phoebe Twinkle was the only one present who'd had no idea what had gone on that day and was agog.

"What about Jack Summer?" Lily asked. "We can't tell him anything, I guess."

"If Jack were interested, he's just as capable as you two were at ferreting out the information I needed," Howard said.

"The Sleuthing Siblings," Robert said. "What do you think of that?"

"Euuw," Howard said.

"You don't like it?"

"I just have an aversion to alliterations. Especially bad ones."

Lily wasn't amused. "I really hate that we pushed ourselves into other people's private lives."

"If you hadn't, two deaths would probably have remained unsolved for much longer," Phoebe said.

"What will happen to Eugene and Mr. White, Elgin?" Mrs. Prinney asked.

He raised his shoulders. "I can't speculate. I've seen too many cases of justice not working as it should. Most often it does. But I'm still astonished that they both confessed so easily. I only had one case before like that, and it was a thug who was bragging about killing his wife. Those who commit crimes of any sort always try to play the innocent."

He sounded a bit put out about this difference and went on, almost bitterly, "I'll have to get a diary and start with today. Because it's never going to happen again."

There was a long raucous blast of horn in the driveway and they all got up to see what was going on. All but Howard Walker, who sat over his coffee, still brooding about his good luck.

A big white truck had pulled in. A man was opening the back doors, and a sturdy woman was putting folding steps up to it. Neither person was familiar to any of them.

"We're the traveling store," the man said. "Mrs. Henry White hired us. Would you like to see what we've got in here?"

Mrs. Prinney was hoisted aboard. She'd broken her cast-iron cornbread mold and was looking for another. Mr. Prinney went inside Grace and Favor, shaking his head. Phoebe joined Mrs. Prinney, hoping to find some material and ribbons for her hats. Robert and Lily took a quick look around, while Agatha barked her head off.

Lily said, "We have nothing to contribute."

"And nothing we need," Robert added. As an aside to Lily, as they headed around the house to sit outside and look over the river, he added, "Maybe the next time it comes around, we could put in chits offering ourselves as private investigators."

Lily ignored this suggestion. When they'd established themselves on the bench where they customarily sat to gaze out over the landscape and talk things over, she said, "I just realized we got it backward."

"Got what backward?"

"You were the one who was working on finding out who the mummy was, and I figured it out."

"And you were overwrought about Roxanne being arrested for her husband's death, and I found the final clues," Robert said. He slapped his head with an exaggerated comic gesture and added, "I guess this proves the old adage that two heads are better than one."

"I think it only proves that we snooped into matters that were none of our business."

"But Lily, Bernard VanZillen will be buried decently instead of in a pauper's grave. And Roxanne won't have to spend the rest of her life worrying that maybe her brother killed her husband—deliberately."

As Lily flounced back to the mansion, she had the last word. "Robert, I just hate it when you say something so intelligent."

*Welcome to the World of
Jill Churchill.
Award-winning, often fun,
and always deadly,
Jill Churchill's world is sure
to keep you guessing.*

Anything Goes

In the first Grace and Favor novel siblings Lily and Robert Brewster, former rich socialites, have become desperately poor after The Crash of '29. Two years later they 'inherit' a mansion from a great-uncle. But it won't be theirs unless they live in it for ten years and make their own living.

"Our great-uncle Horatio was murdered!" Lily exclaimed. "By whom?"

Jack Summer, the town newspaper reporter, had to admire her grammar—and her delivery. She sounded genuinely shocked.

"I don't know. Nobody knows. My editor handled the story himself and I never heard the details." That was a hard admission to make since it made him look like a mere flunky.

"I don't understand why Mr. Prinney didn't tell us this," Robert said. "Somebody actually killed our uncle? On purpose?"

"I couldn't swear to the truth of it," Jack admitted. "But that's what folks in town say."

"Who killed him?" Lily asked.

"Nobody knows. There are only rumors."

The way he was waffling made Robert suspicious. "I think you have everything you need for your interview, don't you?" he said pleasantly.

Jack took the hint, stuffed his notebook and pencil in his pocket, thanked them for their time and departed.

"Why didn't Mr. Prinney tell us this?" Lily asked Robert when Jack Summer had left. They were standing on the porch watching him set off.

"I don't know. Maybe it's just a silly rumor. Mr. Prinney doesn't seem the type to go in for idle gossip," Robert said. "Maybe that's why he clammed up at dinner last night when you asked him about the accident."

"I only asked Mr. Prinney what happened in a general way. He was on board the yacht and people don't like talking about horrible experiences."

"Lily, don't be daft. Most people love talking about horrible experiences. It constitutes the majority of after-dinner talk. Especially among men. And I've overheard women talk about childbirth in terms that make me want to curl up in a ball and whimper. Jack Summer didn't seem to want to talk about it either. He's a reporter. He should have known a lot about it."

"Robert, what are you getting at exactly?"

"Just that I want to know more. And I want to know why nobody will really discuss it with us. You know, Lily, when a man of enormous wealth dies in something called an accident, warning flags should go up everywhere."

"What do you mean?"

"Motives, my dear child."

Lily looked at him patronizingly. "Motives?"

"Since we inherited from him, we have the greatest motive," Robert said. "But we didn't even remember him. At least, I didn't."

"What!"

Robert waved his hands frantically. "No, no. But as far as anyone else knows, in theory we did have a compelling motive. We were about as far down on our luck as a snake on skates and a great-uncle dies in an accident and leaves us his house and fortune. At least, that's what it must look like to people who don't know us."

"But if, as it sounds, he was murdered on the boat, we're obviously in the clear. We weren't there. And we couldn't have afforded to be there if we'd been invited."

"Lily, I'd bet the only person in Voorburg who knows we haven't two beans to rub together is Mr. Prinney. The people of the town don't know that and neither does Jack Sprat."

"Jack Summer," she said, preoccupied. "Do you think Mr. Prinney suspected us? Or maybe still does?"

"Dear God, I hope not! Why would he let us move in here—unless he had in mind a little detecting of his own."

"Robert, lower your voice. The house and yard are full of workers who might be eavesdropping on this bizarre conversation. Let's take a walk."

They strolled, with ostentatious casualness, out in the road in front and pretended to be pointing out plants and wildlife to each other as they spoke in low voices.

"There are other kinds of motives for causing an—accident," Lily said.

"You mean murder."

Lily shuddered. "I don't mean murder, precisely. A rejected lover might have wished to simply alarm someone and went too far. Or a cheated business acquaintance or partner. We don't really know anything about Uncle Horatio. We've been thinking about him as a kindly old gentleman because he gave us this house."

"You might think that indicates kindliness, I'm not sure I do," Robert said with a grin. "Uncle Horatio might have been a real horror. And keep in mind, Lily, that he didn't 'give' us this house. He set it up so we have to be incarcerated here for a whole decade to ever really own it. That doesn't precisely smell of milk and honey. Men who arrange things for other people beyond their own deaths certainly aren't fading violets in life."

In the Still of the Night

Lily and Robert host a party, inviting a famous novel-ist to spend a few days with fans—well-placed re-viewers and readers who will pay for the privilege.

"We still have room for another guest," Lily said. "Several others, in fact, but I think the first time it would be a good idea to keep it to six guests plus the celebrity. That's enough people for pleasant conver-sation with each other, but not a mob. We don't want to scare our first famous person off by having a swarming herd of people demanding his attention. Especially since he's such a reclusive person."

"Aren't you even curious about that?" Robert asked. "Why did Julian West, of all people, agree to this?"

"You sound downright suspicious, Robert."

"I suppose I am, a little. I can't quite put my fin-ger on what motive he might have for coming here, but I don't quite like it."

"Robert, this isn't like you," Lily said, moving his ace of spades to the side of the other cards.

Robert slapped her hand away. "I like keeping it there until I need the space. Maybe I'm just bored into inventing trouble where none exists. How about Mad Henry Trover?"

"As a guest? Mad Henry? This is a joke, isn't it?"

"Mad Henry is fun to have around."

"Mad Henry is a drunk," Lily said.

"He doesn't drink at all," Robert said. "He just has a naturally exuberant personality. I like Mad Henry. Always did."

"Does he still have money?" Lily asked.

"Wads. Tons. It falls out of his pockets and rolls across floors. People follow him around picking it up. His father discovered that gold mine, you remember, then considerately dropped dead so Mad Henry could have his toys. The villagers at the village fete will love him."

"I don't imagine Mad Henry knows what a novel is."

"Probably not, but I'd enjoy catching up with him," Robert said.

Mad Henry considered himself an inventor and always had one or another peculiar project that he was engaged in. Lily found Henry annoying and remembered vividly the time he'd visited them for the summer in Nantucket and decided to rewire the house with something he claimed was a new metal of his own creation. It took the whole family, staff and several neighbors with buckets of seawater to put the fire out.

"He's given up anything to have to do with combustion, I hear," Robert said, laying out a new hand of patience. "I think there must be a card missing. I can't seem to win."

He sounded so pathetic that Lily gave in. "All right, invite Mad Henry. But you're in charge of him if he gets out of hand."

Robert grinned. "He's really smart, you know. Most of his projects don't work out, but someday he'll invent something good."

"Better than the suspenders?"

"He didn't think he invented suspenders. He just made them easier to pack," Robert said, laughing. "Instead of them getting all tangled up, they were a series of stiffened wood bits that could be folded up neatly like a carpenter's rule. Ands what's more, you could change the color just by painting them."

She liked it when Robert laughed. He'd always been so good-natured and since they'd come here, he was marginally less cheerful. If it took putting up with Mad Henry to make him happy taking in a bunch of intellectual guests that would probably bore him senseless, so be it.

Someone To Watch Over Me

Robert decides to tear down the old ice house out in the woods around Grace and Favor Cottage and gets quite a surprise.

"Lily, guess what we found in the old ice-house?"

"A million dollars?" Lily asked.

"Nope. Guess again."

"Oh, Robert. You know I'll never guess."

"A body."

"Hmm. A body of what? A possum? A fox?"

"Lily, you're so unimaginative. The body of a man."

Lily hugged herself as if protecting herself from the news. "A man? Who? Haven't we already had enough deaths here?"

"This isn't a recent one. It's more like a mummy."

"An old Indian or something?"

"Not quite. A very well-dressed gentleman."

The town's reporter Jack Summer had quietly approached and startled Lily when he said, "Where is he?"

"Already on his way to Albany," Robert said.

"Whew," Jack said. "I was afraid Doc Polhemus would be involved. He's such a fool and a gossip." Jack was often one of the people Dr. Polhemus brought up by name when he blathered about his wart theory, claiming he'd cured Jack and others of warts by identifying and destroying what he called The Mother Wart. It always made Jack mad to have this secret shared in public.

"We all know that," Robert said. "Sheriff Walker took care that Dr. Polhemus didn't know about it until he'd contacted the coroner up there. Polhemus is out of town for a couple of days and a brand new doctor from Fishkill is filling in for him. Walker told the substitute the man could have been from anywhere. Not necessarily local. Walker asked the State of New York to step in."

"Lily," Jack said, "don't you have something to do?"

"What?" she asked, still trying to absorb the bad news.

"The Bonus March," Jack said. "Remember?"

"Oh, yes." Lily hurried inside.

"Do you really have no idea whose body it is?" Jack asked when Lily was apparently out of hearing range.

"I've only lived here for a short time. And this guy's been dead for a long time," Robert replied.

"Oh, wasn't he just a skeleton in clothing?"

"No, I told you that he was like a mummy. I guess because the old icehouse was so sturdy and well chinked and probably closed up when the air was very dry." Robert thought for a moment.

"Maybe he was put in there in very cold, dry weather and froze solid."

"Couldn't anyone else identify him?"

"There were only the Harbinger brothers helping me take down the icehouse. And—" Robert paused, trying to think of a tactful way to explain.

"And what?" Jack demanded.

"His face is unrecognizable. Hands as well. The only parts of him that were exposed. Mice probably."

Jack turned a little bit green. "I see. Did Howard Walker have any guess how long he'd been there?"

"Nope. I don't know how anyone could tell. If Uncle Horatio was still using the icehouse, the body probably wasn't out there until after he died. Or maybe not. Grace and Favor stood vacant for quite a while after Great-uncle Horatio died."

"But was it still in use when he was alive? When was the ice storage shed added to the side of the pantry?"

Robert scratched his head. "Again, it was here when we arrived. Might have been put on years or even decades ago."

"Who would know?" Jack nagged.

"I have no idea. Great-uncle Horatio's dead. His staff, which was small, all came along with him when his Aunt Flora died. I assume they all went back to wherever they came from. There wasn't anyone around but hoboes when we came here. And they all lived in the kitchen."

"So there isn't anyone who would remember who we could find?"

"Probably not. Why do you care so much about dates?" Robert asked.

"Well, obviously it's local news and I'm the editor of the paper. But how long the body could have been there would be a clue as to who it might be. If, for example, the new icehouse was built onto the pantry in 1920, the body could have been put in the old one in the woods anytime after that. So you'd have a long list of men it might be. If it was much later, you cut down on the possibilities."

"Hmm. I hadn't thought of it that way. Are you going to investigate the murder?"

"Murder! You didn't say it was a murder!" Jack exclaimed.

Robert ran his hands through his normally well-groomed hair in frustration. "I figure it had to be. He was bashed on the back of the head and laid out very formally with his hands on his chest, tied lightly together with some sort of string. I don't think you could consider it suicide or a natural death."

Love for Sale

The Brewsters have guests again but not ones of their own choosing. Only days before the election of President Roosevelt a mysterious group wants to have a private meeting. And they'll pay well to have it at Grace and Favor Cottage. Lily doesn't like the idea.

The debate at dinner defeated Lily. "We're supposed to be earning our own living," Robert pointed out. "And if this five hundred dollars is only part of what they'll pay, who cares who they are?"

Mr. Prinney, Esquire, the executor of their great-uncle's estate who'd moved into Grace and Favor with his wife to see that the Brewsters observed the peculiar rules of their inheritance, was on Robert's side as well.

An elderly and prissy lawyer, Mr. Prinney said, "If they want complete privacy, it's to our advantage. What we don't know about their business can't hurt us, and we can't be held responsible. And they probably are quite respectable people who just want to work out something away from prying eyes at their normal office. Lots of highly placed business executives can still afford to take their top people to out-of-the-way places to plan things. Takeovers and such."

Even Mrs. Prinney took up the theory. "Lily, I suspect you're letting your imagination run away with you. Maybe it's his real name. Maybe he's bald and wears a wig because he wants to look younger than he is. We wouldn't have to do anything with them but take up their meals to the big bedroom."

"Mrs. Prinney is right," Robert chimed in. "It's not as if we'd have to socialize with them and feed them in the dining room with us. I could get the Harbinger boys to dismantle one of the tables stored in the basement to take up to the bedroom. They'd like to be paid to do it."

Only Phoebe Twinkle, their own milliner and seamstress boarder, was on Lily's side and knew she had no real right to interfere and kept silent during the discussion. But she took Lily aside after dinner and said, "I think Robert and Mr. Prinney should take the food up. They shouldn't even see Mimi, Mrs. Prinney or the two of us."

"You think they're gangsters, too?"

"Not really. I think Mr. Prinney's right. They might even be politicians, planning something for this election. That's my theory. Maybe with the vote for president coming up, they're Hoover's men trying to come up with a frantic last minute plan to get him in. Or, I hate to say it, but they might be Reds planning to disrupt the election."

She started upstairs to do some of her sewing, but stopped and added, "But the women in the house shouldn't be involved except maybe for the extra cooking."

"Are you worried at being on the same floor with the other men?" Lily asked.

"Not at all. The bedroom doors all have good locks, and so do the bathrooms. Put them all at the end that has the men's bathroom, though. It's farther from the stairs so Mimi and I can dart into our bathroom without running into them."

"Good idea."

"It's only for a few days and lots of money," Phoebe said with an encouraging smile. "Now I must go upstairs and put the finishing touch on Mrs. Roosevelt's hat she ordered for the inauguration. Did I tell you what she said about it?"

"No."

"That she never wanted and still doesn't want to be a First Lady. Poor dear."

Murder Is on the Menu
at the Hillside Manor Inn
Bed-and-Breakfast Mysteries by
MARY DAHEIM
featuring Judith McMonigle Flynn